All I really knew about my father was that he was a tall, skinny, and near-sighted man my mother claimed to love. Getting Mom to talk about him was almost as improbable as the star quarterback asking me out on a date. She flat out refused to discuss him. There were no pictures of my father; according to her she didn't own any. I couldn't imagine how she didn't have *any* pictures of him, but that was her story, and throughout my childhood and adolescence, she stuck to it like a drowning man clutches to a life jacket.

What she did own of my father's was a pair of old, scratched-up glasses. They were black horn-rims – the type all librarians from Hell wore. Part of me fantasized that my father looked like Malcolm X. With those old glasses, and my reddish-brown hair and skinny build, it wasn't hard to imagine.

A RED POLKA DOT IN A WORLD FULL OF PLAID

VARIAN JOHNSON

Genesis Press Inc.

Black Coral

An imprint of Genesis Press Inc.
Publishing Company

Genesis Press, Inc.
P.O. Box 101
Columbus, MS 39703

ISBN: 1-58571-140-3
Manufactured in the United States of America

First Edition

Visit us at www.genesis-press.com
or call at 1-888-Indigo-1

DEDICATION

To my parents, Larry and Mildred; to my wife, Crystal;
and to all the Dekes and Maxines out there in the world,
this novel is respectfully dedicated.

ACKNOWLEDGMENTS

First of all, I must thank God, because without him I am nothing. I must thank my parents, Larry and Mildred Johnson; my brother, Brad; and sister, Andrea; and all the rest of my family (those far…and away). Without you guys, I would not be the man I am today (so if I do something wrong, it's all your faults).

There are so many friends to thank, I don't even know where to start. YT Beauford, Tommy Leroy, Necie, Big Mac—thanks for always being there when I needed you guys. An ICE COLD thank you goes out to the distinguished men of the Zeta Zeta Chapter of Alpha Phi Alpha Fraternity, Inc., especially that frozen line of Fall '97—Orlando "Frenchie" Chapple, Shun "the Seventeen Dollar Super-H" Casey, Corey "Texas Gator" Ellis, Lucious "Wave Rider" Selmon, Brad "Frank Sinatra" Johnson, and Rodney "Rev. Rose" Connally. You guys helped me through the trials and tribulations of college life, and beyond. To my agents, Sharene Martin and Robert Brown, thanks for believing in me when few others did. Thank you to the Words of Wisdom Writers' Society (Del, Paula, Tahiti 3000, Trina, Victor, Grace, Adele and everyone else) for taking me in, accepting me as one of your own, and helping to make my dreams come true. Thanks to the entire staff at Genesis Press for putting up with my constant barrage of questions, and for safely ushering me into the world of publishing.

And finally, to my favorite girl, the one that keeps me straight when the world looks crooked, Crystal—thanks for just being you.

If I missed anyone (and I'm sure I did) don't take it personally; you know how I am.

CHAPTER 1

"Why didn't you tell me?"

Mom was leaning over the sink, her hands submerged in soapy water. "Maxine, what are you talking about?"

I tightened my grip on the cordless phone. "You know exactly what I'm talking about!"

Her head snapped up. She spun around so fast, suds flew from her fingertips and splashed against my face. "How dare you use that tone of voice with—"

"My tone of voice?" I tried to stop myself from shaking. I didn't know whether to laugh or scream. Instead, I hurled the phone against the wall and watched its plastic pieces scatter across the linoleum.

"Girl, what the hell is your problem?" Mom screamed as she charged toward me.

"Why didn't you tell me my father was still alive?"

She froze. "What—what are you talking about?"

"Who do you think that last call was from?"

Wrinkles shot into my mother's mahogany-colored skin. Suddenly she looked a lot older than her forty-two years. "He called?"

"I see you're not denying it now." I turned and began to march out.

"Maxine Edrice Phillips, don't even *think* about walking out of this room."

I jerked to a stop. As much as I hated to admit it, Mom's voice always had a certain power over me. It was like a leash, yanking me back to reality.

"Let me explain," she said, in a softer voice.

I crossed my arms. "Yeah Mom, please explain how in eighteen years, you couldn't find the time to tell me he was alive."

"I was only trying to protect you."

"Protect me? Don't I have the right to know who my father is?"

She frowned. "Don't raise your voice at me."

"The hell with my voice—"

Her hand was across my face before I could finish my statement. The slap was cold and quick, and so strong I almost lost my balance.

A quiet iciness settled around us. Mom stared at me, in the loudest silence I had ever experienced. Her hand lingered in the air as if she was going to hit me again. Her eyes were so intense, I couldn't bear to look at them.

For the first time ever, I felt uncomfortable around my mother. Of course, maybe she wasn't my mother after all. My mother would never lie to me or slap me.

I couldn't take the silence any longer. I stormed toward the door.

"Where are you going?" she yelled after me.

I didn't bother to turn around. "Out!"

A cool summer breeze struck my hot cheek as I headed toward my magic carpet on wheels, a lime green hatchback Hyundai. I started the car and tried to ignore Mom's gaze as she stood in the doorway.

I could still feel her eyes on me, as I pulled out of the driveway and sped down the street.

Deke's mother opened the door and stared at me. I hated to imagine how I looked. I could feel my cherry-brown, frizzled hair pointing in all directions. In my too-old, too-baggy sweats, I probably looked like Medusa in an aerobics video.

"Maxine, come in," she said as she ushered me inside. Suitcases and bags were scattered across the den. Deke's stepfather was in the process of trying to force one of the suitcases to close. He looked up as I entered the room.

"Maxine," he said. "How much do you weigh?"

"What?"

"Never mind, just come over here and sit on this suitcase."

Great—not only was I ugly and crazy, but I was also fat.

"Jason, will you leave Maxine alone? I'm sure she didn't come here to help you pack." Deke's mother wrapped her arm around my shoulder and gave me a small squeeze. "Deke is in his room."

I left Mr. Ashland struggling with the zipper and walked down the hallway to Deke's room. I could hear him mumbling from behind the door. I tried to press down my hair before knocking.

Immediately the talking stopped and he opened the door. Deke's frame took up most of the doorway. His dark, chocolate skin was like the photo negative of my own khaki-toned complexion. Deke always joked about me being the only girl that reminded him of a pair of pants.

A seemingly concerned frown came to his face. He pressed his lips together and looked me up and down, like he was checking to make sure I was okay. His gaze hovered at my face, on my cheek.

I shrugged.

He nodded as if he understood everything, and let me into the room.

I pushed the pillows off his bed and collapsed onto the marshmallow mattress. "You won't believe the day I've had."

He held his finger up. "Hold on for a second," he said. He picked up the phone receiver lying on his desk. "Yvonne, can I call you back?" A frown came to his face. "Yes, it's her." Another pause. "What do you mean, don't bother calling you back?" By now, I could hear yelling on the other end of the phone. "Of course you're as important to me as— Hello?"

Deke sighed and hung up the phone. "What were you saying?"

"Listen, I can come back later—"

"She'll get over it," he said as he dropped beside me on the bed. "Tell me what happened."

Good old Deke. Just sitting next to him made me feel calmer. He was the closest thing I had to a best friend; probably the closest thing I had to a friend at all.

It had been almost thirteen years since I first met Deke. Mom and I had recently moved from New York to Columbia, South Carolina. I remembered being dragged to my new kindergarten class in an ugly pink dress I didn't want to wear. As the teacher announced my name and as I walked to my seat, all the other kids laughed and pointed at me. I was pale and awkward, with a funny-shaped head, rust-colored hair, and that abominable pink dress didn't help. Later that day, I saw Deke reading a book in the corner. He looked over at me and frowned as if he didn't know what I was. Finally he came over and handed me a book. We had been inseparable ever since.

I looked at Deke. "My father is alive."

His mouth dropped open. At least I wasn't the only one surprised. "Are you sure?"

I nodded.

"What do you know about him?"

"Nothing much," I said. "Just that he and Mom split up when I was about a year old."

Deke became quiet, and I knew he was thinking about his father. Not Jason Ashland, the man who raised him, but his biological father—the man who ran out on Deke and his mother years ago.

"I wish I knew why he left," I said. "I mean, I'm sure there's a good reason." I ignored the grimace on Deke's face. "Anyway, he's pretty much stayed out of our lives until now. He would sometimes call every few years, but that was about it. But a few weeks ago, he called Mom and said that he wanted to meet me."

"After all this time?"

I nodded. "Mom didn't think it was a good idea, so he decided to call me himself. Unfortunately, I hung up on him before we could really talk about anything."

"Why did you hang up on him?"

"I was nervous. I didn't know what to say, what to think, or what to do. I didn't even believe he was telling the truth until I confronted Mom."

Deke paced the small room. "You know, your mother called for you. She told me about the…altercation y'all had." He picked up the phone. "You have to call her."

"I don't *have* to do anything." I fought the temptation to rub my tender cheek. "Are your parents ready for their trip?" I asked.

He nodded. "Beginning tomorrow night, I'll have two whole weeks to myself."

"You mean, you and Yvonne will have two whole weeks to yourselves," I said with a smirk.

"Nope. I'm taking a break from everyone, including her."

I smiled. For any ordinary eighteen-year-old, two weeks without any parental supervision would be an everyday prom night, without the dinner and fancy dresses. But knowing Deke, he would spend the entire time watching cartoons and eating cereal.

"Stop trying to change the subject." He still had the phone in his hand. "Are you going to talk to your mother?"

"She slapped me, Deke. Am I supposed to forget that?"

He sighed, and his voice grew quiet. "Maybe you deserved it."

I jumped from the bed and got in his face. "I know you didn't say that."

He took a step back. "Maxine, she's your mother. She deserves a certain amount of respect."

I pouted, but I knew he was right. I had never cursed at my mother before. I never had any reason to, until today.

Wait a minute. She was the one who hit me. Why did I feel guilty? I finally rubbed my cheek. She must have knocked something loose with that slap.

Again he extended the phone to me. "Call her."

I shook my head. What did he want me to do, thank her for slapping me?

"Didn't you and Yvonne break up a couple of weeks ago?" I glanced around the room for pictures of her, but there were none. There was one of Deke and his family, and one of me. That was it.

"I see there's no point in arguing with you." Deke dropped the phone back on his desk. "Yeah, we broke up, but we got back together."

"You know what your problem is?" I didn't wait for a response. "You need to have sex."

Deke frowned. "You know I can't do that."

"Why not? It's not hard to do. Just get naked and—"

"I don't need lessons." He picked up the two pillows I had pushed to the floor and returned them to the bed. "Anyway, at least I have a girlfriend. I don't see any guys beating down your door."

Good point.

"No guy in his right mind would ask me out. I mean, look at me. I'm a skinny black girl with gray eyes and hair that has a mind of its own."

My skin tone was what some people called "high yellow." My hair had been a bane my entire life, always pointing every which way except the way I wanted. It constantly changed colors during the year, from an almost respectable reddish-brown hue in the winter to an embarrassing strawberry-red, burnt-orange, cherry-brown mix in the summer. Deke would try to make me feel better by describing me as "exotic." I just considered myself a freak of nature.

"Why are you so hard on yourself?" Deke asked. "You're very pretty."

Yeah, easy for him to say. Deke had the physique of an overpaid pro-football player. Half the girls in town had a crush on him. The other half was either blind, stupid, or insane. I included myself in the insane category.

"So when are you going to talk to your mother?"

I smirked. "The day after never?"

"You have to go home eventually."

I ran my fingers through Deke's thick, curly hair and leaned close to his ear. "I figured you and I would just run off, shack up, and have a couple of illegitimate children."

Deke crossed his arms.

"Or, maybe not."

It was almost midnight by the time I returned home. I gently unlocked the back door and crept into the house. I hoped Mom was asleep, because the last thing I needed was to get into another argument with her. I was doing fine until the floor squeaked underneath me.

"Maxine, is that you?"

Mom appeared from her room and walked down the hallway. Katherine Phillips was, by far, the most beautiful woman I knew. Where I stood awkwardly, she stood gracefully. Where I stuttered, she sang. Her eyes were a soft hazel, not a hard gray, and her jet black hair looked like it was spun of silk. Her smooth, brown skin shimmered in the artificial light of the kitchen.

"I see you're finally home," she said. "I was worried about you."

"I'll bet."

Mom seemed to ignore my comment. She pulled out a chair from the table and sat. "The way you ran out of the house, I—"

"Don't you understand? I don't want to talk to you."

Mom's face became long. "You probably think I'm the most evil person in the world, but believe me when I say my intentions were good."

"So lying is okay now. I knew those Ten Commandments weren't all they were cracked up to be."

"Maxine, you can't possibly understand—"

"No, I understand. You were so wrapped up in your feelings, you couldn't bother to tell me that my father was alive and that he wanted to meet me," I said. "And when I did ask about him, you slapped me. I think that's about all I can stomach for tonight."

Before she could respond, I ran into my room and slammed the door shut. In my mind, I could still see Mom sitting at the table with that same expression on her face. I thought yelling at her would make me feel better. I was mistaken.

I looked in the mirror. There was still the slightest hint of redness to my face. One of the downfalls of having light skin was that it bruised extremely easily.

I heard a chair scrape along the kitchen floor and footsteps travel down the hallway. They stopped in front of my room.

I walked back to my door and placed my trembling hand on the knob. I was unsure whether I should open it or leave it closed. I listened. Finally, the footsteps moved away. After a few more moments of silence, I opened the door. All that remained in the hallway was a small note. It had Jack Phillips's name on it. And his number.

As I picked the note up and walked back to my bed, I couldn't help staring at the faded slip of paper. After taking a few deep breaths, I picked up the phone. I hurriedly dialed the number, before I lost my nerve.

The phone rang.

What if I'm making a mistake? He could be asleep. Or what if he's married and I wake up his wife? Or what if—

"Hello, this is Jack."

I paused, trying to force the words out of my mouth.

"Hello?" the voice said on the other end of the phone. "Is anyone there?"

"Um...hi," I stammered. "This is Maxine Phillips, your daughter."

CHAPTER 2

I stared at Deke out of the corner of my eye and waited for him to speak. He sat on his couch, in a frayed t-shirt and a pair of old gym shorts. A bowl of soggy bran flakes sat in his lap.

Deke slowly chewed and swallowed before turning to me. "You called him?"

I nodded. "We didn't talk for long, though. He lives in Oklahoma, in a little town called Chickasha. He works at the local hospital."

"How did your father end up in Oklahoma?"

"I don't know, we didn't get that far." I closed my eyes and thought back to last night. "He's a deacon at a church there."

"At least he has one good thing going for him."

I rolled my eyes. "I don't care if he's the Pope. No one is changing my mind about God anytime soon."

"Don't you think it was an act of God that brought you and your father together?"

"I thought it was a phone call. Does God work for Bell South?"

Deke shoveled the last of his cereal into his mouth. "Can you even try to listen to what I have to say about God without making some type of smart remark?"

"Is that a trick question?" I asked as I looked at my reflection in the glass coffee table. "I wonder how much I look like him?"

"Does that matter?"

"Of course it matters," I said. "I had to get this screwed up body from someone."

"Maybe you'll get the chance to meet him after a few months."

"A few months? It's already July. In a few months I'll be in college." I stole a glance at Deke. "Maybe I could go visit him now."

"Now? Are you crazy?" Deke jumped up, knocking his empty bowl to the floor. "This is the first time you've heard from the guy in eighteen years."

"But—"

"What do you know about him? Is he married? Does he have a girlfriend? Does he have a boyfriend?"

I frowned at Deke. "Not funny."

"Does he have any other children?"

Good question. I wondered if there were any other gray-eyed, light-skinned black kids running around the prairie out there.

"Anyway, your mother would never dream of letting you visit him so soon."

"If it was up to her, she wouldn't let me visit him at all."

"And what's so wrong with that? He left once. Let him stay gone."

I eyed Deke. "Don't start."

"Did you ask him why he left?" he asked.

"No," I said. "It's not important."

"Not important? You have to be at least somewhat curious."

Saying I was "somewhat curious" could have been the understatement of the year. I had hundreds of questions for my father, with number one being, "Why did you leave?" But as much as I had tried the night before, I couldn't bring myself to ask him that question for one reason: I didn't know if I could stomach his reply.

"How far is Oklahoma from here, anyhow?" Deke asked, bringing me back to the present.

"I asked him last night. He said that it takes about eighteen hours to drive."

Deke leaned back and stroked the invisible hairs on his chin. "Do you hear yourself?"

"What are you talking about?"

"Almost every time you make reference to your father, you say 'he' instead of his name."

I sighed. That boy was too observant for his own good. "I don't know what to call him. I don't want to call him Jack, but I can't call him Dad. At least not yet."

He shrugged. "At least you can call him something."

All I really knew about my father was that he was a tall, skinny, and near-sighted man my mother claimed to love. Getting Mom to talk about him was almost as improbable as the star quarterback asking me out on a date. She flat out refused to discuss him. There were no pictures of my father; according to her she didn't own any. I couldn't imagine how she didn't have *any* pictures of him, but that was her story, and throughout my childhood and adolescence, she stuck to it like a drowning man clutches to a life jacket.

What she did own of my father's was a pair of old, scratched-up glasses. They were black horn-rims—the type all librarians from Hell wore. Part of me fantasized that my father looked like Malcolm X. With those old glasses, and my reddish-brown hair and skinny build, it wasn't hard to imagine.

As much as Mom avoided talking about Jack Phillips, there were times when she would slip and say something about him. Maybe a song would be playing on the radio and she would casually comment, "Jack used to like that song." Or maybe as she flipped channels, she would stop at a baseball game and would almost whisper, "The Dodgers. Jack loved the Dodgers." I felt like a cactus sometimes, with each piece of information like a drop of water that would have to sustain me until Mom spoke of my father again. As I sat across from her and ate my dinner, I was in desperate need of a few drops of that nourishment now.

"I called him," I said. Those were the first words I had said to her since last night.

Mom didn't respond immediately. Instead, she rose from the table and carried her plate to the sink. The way she walked across the kitchen, you would think she was in a funeral procession.

"You would have found his number even if I hadn't given it to you," she finally said. "I figured I'd just save you the time."

I walked to her with slow, careful steps. "It was good talking to him. I was nervous at first, but after a while we warmed up to each other. We got along so well, I was thinking…maybe I could visit him this summer."

"No," Mom said, not bothering to look at me.

"Why not?" I asked. "He's my father, isn't he? Why can't a girl visit her own father?"

"Honey, you just spoke to him for the first time yesterday."

"If you had told me the truth—"

"Don't start this again, Maxine."

"But Mom—"

She spun around and planted her hands on her hips. "I'm not going to argue about this. There are a lot of things you don't know about Jack Phillips."

"Like what?"

Mom frowned. "It's complicated, Maxine. Let's talk about it in a few days. Anyway, you need to be focusing on getting ready for college."

"It's not like I'm going to school in Alaska. Clemson is just a few hours away."

"Yes, but this will be your first time away from home."

"No big deal. I can take care of myself."

"Oh, really?"

"Yes, really." I hated it when Mom talked to me like I was a baby. I was basically a grown woman. All I needed now was a good job, lots of money, and some breasts. Shouldn't be too hard to get.

"We're not talking about me and college, remember. We're talking about me visiting my father."

"How could I forget?" she said. "Maybe he can visit during Thanksgiving break."

Thanksgiving break? She couldn't be serious.

Mom crossed her arms and stared me down. "And that's final."

Okay, maybe she was serious.

Mom yawned and handed me a dishtowel. "I'm tired. Finish cleaning up the kitchen."

"I should have known better than to try to talk to you," I mumbled as I dropped the silverware into the sink.

Mom stopped walking and turned back around. "And just what does that mean?" she asked.

"Forget it," I said. I turned on the faucet.

Mom wasn't letting me off that easily, though. She marched over to me and turned the water off. "Maxine, what did you mean by that?"

"It means you never talk to me!" I yelled. "You're always too busy, or too tired or—"

"Dammit, I work twelve hours a day. I deserve to be tired." She pointed a finger at me. "You need to grow up and stop being so selfish. Contrary to what you believe, the world does not revolve around you."

"Selfish?" I said. "You're the one that didn't tell me about my father. If that isn't selfish, I don't know what is!"

Mom looked like she was going to explode. "Maxine, I let you get away with this crap yesterday, but don't think I'm going to let you talk down to me like that on a daily basis. I'm the one that bought you that car outside. I'm the one paying for you to go to college. Little girl, I'm the Momma around here—you're the child. You'd better remember that."

She disappeared down the hallway and left me in the kitchen to clean up. This was how most evenings ended. Not with an argument, but with me in the kitchen by myself and Mom in her room or in her study, working.

If there was one thing my mother was, it was a hard worker. She put herself through law school with a full-time baby girl, a full-time job, and full-time bills weighing her down. She eventually worked her way up from an entry-level associate position to a partner at her firm. Mom worked every day, even Christmas. She was dedicated to her job and to providing for all my needs and wants. But all the clothes and toys in the world didn't make up for the birthday parties she had to miss, the Girl Scout cookies she couldn't help me sell, and the countless weekends I spent alone.

As I began washing dishes, I couldn't help thinking about her attitude toward my father. Why was she so dead set against me meeting him? Maybe she was jealous. All of a sudden she had to share me with someone else, and she couldn't handle it.

Well, I didn't care what Mom thought. One way or the other I was going to meet Jack Phillips.

"I really enjoy talking to you," I whispered. It was almost one in the morning and I didn't want Mom to hear me on the phone, especially with my father.

"I was wondering…" I began, before letting my words drift off. I felt like a dam that was about to burst. I took a deep breath. "Can I visit you out there?" I finally blurted out.

I held my breath for what seemed like hours waiting for him to respond. *Please say yes, please say yes, please say —*

"I'd love for you to come out here and visit me."

"Really?" I could feel myself beaming.

"Yes, really."

I felt like I was dreaming. After all this time, I was finally going to meet my father.

"As soon as your mother okays it, you can fly out."

My mother? Damn, some dream. Who woke me up?

"It's getting late," he said. "We'd better hang up."

"Are you sure? I'm not tired at all," I said, although I could hardly keep my eyes open.

"I'm sure. Good night, Maxine."

"Good night…Jack."

There was a pause on the other end of the phone. I hoped I hadn't offended him by calling him by his first name.

"Good night," he said again, and hung up.

As I turned off the lamp, I wondered what he looked like. It would be nice to be around someone who actually looked like me. Maybe I would finally fit in somewhere.

Yeah, I could see him in six months.

I sat up and turned the lamp back on.

Or maybe I could see him sooner.

"Goodbye, Mom." I waved to her as she pulled out of the driveway.

She waved back and disappeared down the street. As soon as she was out of sight, I rushed back inside and grabbed my suitcase from the top of my closet. I dragged it from my room and threw it into the trunk of the car. I slammed the trunk shut, sending specks of rust across myself.

I didn't bother to brush the rust from my clothes. Instead, I ran back into the house and grabbed the atlas from the bookshelf. I traced the snake-like route from South Carolina to Oklahoma with my finger and committed it to memory. I shrugged. It didn't look that bad.

I picked up the phone and dialed Jack's number. After four rings, I hung up. *Maybe he's at work. I'll call him when I stop for the night.*

I immediately dialed Deke's number. As the phone rang, I thought about the conversation we had had the day before. Maybe Deke was right about God bringing Jack and me together after all this time. Maybe God had finally found the time to answer my prayers.

"Hello," Deke said. He sounded like his mouth was full of peanut butter.

"Deke, it's me. I'm gonna do it."

"That's nice, talk to you later."

I rolled my eyes. "You don't even know what I'm talking about, do you?"

There was a pause. "Um, yeah I do. You're talking about...."

"Deke, I'm going to Oklahoma to visit my father."

He yawned. "Yeah, just what I said."

I sighed. It was six in the morning. You'd think he'd be up.

"Tell Mom I'm sorry and that I'll call her when I stop for the night."

"Yeah, whatever." He hung up the phone.

I hoped he would remember everything I told him. I looked around the house once more before walking outside and locking the door.

Although it was the middle of July, it wasn't overbearingly hot. The last remnants of dew still clung to the grass in the yard.

I stared at my house. It wasn't terribly big, but it provided more than enough room for me and Mom.

I wondered how Jack's house looked. I pictured a big, two-story house overlooking a quiet brook. I could almost smell the fresh straw-berries in the air from the backyard garden. I could almost taste the sweet watermelon juice sliding down my throat.

I stopped daydreaming and climbed into the car. After a few pumps of the gas pedal, the lime green magic carpet once again purred to life.

Oklahoma, here I come.

CHAPTER 3

"Girl, where are you? Don't you know your mother is worried sick about you!"

I held the phone away from my ear as Deke yelled into the other end. After a few seconds of silence, I placed the receiver back to my ear.

"I'm in Alabama."

"Alabama!"

I sighed. "My car stopped along I-20. I think it overheated."

"Didn't you check the fluids in your car before you left?"

"Oops."

I could imagine the scowl on Deke's face. "Where are you, specifically?" he asked.

"I'm in a town called Cottondale, at a corner store."

"Give me the phone number and I'll call you back in a few minutes," he said. "I'll call your mother and—"

"No! Don't call her."

"Don't call her? How do you expect to get back?"

I smiled. "Well, I was hoping…"

"Don't even say it."

"But Deke—"

"There is no way I'm driving to Alabama."

I looked at my watch and counted. 5…4…3…2…

He sighed. "Give me the directions. I'll be there in a few hours."

I recognized Deke's car the moment I saw it. It was all I could do to contain myself from running into the street and tackling it. He slowed down and pulled into the parking lot.

"I can't believe I let you convince me to come all the way out here," Deke said as he stepped out of his car.

Boy, he sure did look a lot bigger when he was angry.

I backed away from him as he neared me. "I know you're probably kinda mad right now, but I can explain everything."

"Where's your car?"

I pointed across the street. "I had a guy tow it from the interstate to his garage. He said that I overheated the engine and warped something or other. I figured you could talk to him, since you know so much about cars."

"Okay, let's go talk to him."

"The only problem is, he won't be back in until tomorrow."

Deke snorted. "I guess that means we're stuck here for the night."

I picked up my bag. "Afraid so."

Deke was grinding his teeth so hard, I could almost see his molars turning into powder. "Get in the car," he said. "Let's find someplace to stay."

Deke opened the door to the room and walked in. I followed behind him. Instantly, a wave of must hit my face and almost knocked me to the floor.

"I can't believe this is the only motel in this town with a vacancy," I said as I walked to the window. "And look at this. We have a great view of the strip club across the street." I stared at a woman and a man on the corner. After a few seconds of watching what I considered very public displays of affection, I closed the blinds.

"I don't think anyone has used this room in a long time," he said as he sat on one of the beds.

"What gave it away? The stench of the room, or the cobwebs hanging from the ceiling?" I walked into the bathroom and turned on the faucet. "Just curious, is this supposed to be brown or have I been drinking the wrong color water all my life?"

Deke came into the bathroom and watched as the murky water flowed into the sink. He threw his hands into the air. "Outstanding."

"At least it's not black."

We returned to the main room. Deke picked up a phone book and began flipping through it. "Does pizza sound okay?" He stopped on a page and brought his face closer to the book. "Here's a restaurant that specializes in hamburgers, pizzas, gyros, and bagels. And they deliver."

As he dialed the number, I walked to the air conditioner. The hot, damp air seemed to have followed us into the room. It was so humid, I felt like I was carrying a second layer of skin. I turned up the air conditioner and stood in front of the vent. I unfastened one of the buttons on my shirt and spread my arms. I could feel the drops of sweat rolling down my back and seeping into my shirt. As I loosened another button and pulled my shirt out of my shorts, I closed my eyes and tried to imagine myself immersed in a cold bath.

"The pizza should be here in about thirty minutes," Deke said as his voice came closer to me. "I ordered pepperoni and…."

I opened my eyes. Deke's gaze was darting everywhere except on me.

"Are you okay?" I asked.

He awkwardly pointed to my chest. "Maybe you should button that up."

I looked down at my chest. The top portion of my bra was exposed. I looked back at Deke. His face was turning purple, which was pretty amazing since his skin was so dark. "Don't tell me you're blushing. You act like you've never seen a bra before."

"It's not the bra I'm looking at."

"Please, I wasn't showing that much cleavage." I pushed past him and buttoned my shirt back up. "I don't have that much to show in the first place."

"Believe me, it's enough." He nodded toward the phone. "You should call your mother."

I stretched out across a bed. The mattress was so hard, it felt like I was lying on granite. "Can't you talk to her for me?" I asked.

"You know I can't." He picked up the phone and dialed my number. "You should probably know, I called her before I came out here."

I bolted up. "What? I told you not to."

"Your mother would have gone crazy worrying about you if I didn't tell her something. I told her that your car broke down and I was coming to pick you up and bring you back home." He finished dialing the number and handed me the phone.

Mom picked it up on the first ring.

"Maxine, what in the hell is wrong with you?" she screamed into the phone. "What were you thinking by pulling a stunt like this?"

"Mom, I'm sorry. I—"

"Did Jack talk you into this?"

"No, ma'am. It was all my idea."

"You may be eighteen, but you're still not too big for me to put a switch to your behind."

I rolled my eyes. "Mom, I'm ten pounds heavier and two inches taller than you."

"Don't be a smartass, Maxine." She sighed. "How could you be so selfish?"

"Selfish? I'm not—"

"Don't start; I don't want to hear it," she snapped. "I'm so mad at you right now, I don't even want to talk to you. Put Deke on the phone."

I kicked Deke's leg and handed him the phone. While he talked to Mom, I flipped through the phone book, trying to ignore their conversation. After fifteen minutes, the pizza arrived, but he remained on the phone. Just as I finished paying the delivery boy, Deke hung up.

"You think you talked long enough?" I asked as I flipped the box open.

Why did this pizza remind me of the delivery boy's face?

"Maxine, your mother is very upset with you, and you really can't blame her. This is by far the most irresponsible thing you've ever done."

I grabbed a slice of pizza and sat beside him. "Don't rub it in. I feel guilty enough already."

Deke smiled and brushed an orphaned strand of hair out of my face. "Don't worry, she'll get over it."

I don't know how to explain it, but as his hand touched the side of my face, I felt a little tingle. The last time I had a feeling like that was when I had a crush on my eighth grade history teacher, Mr. Jenkins.

Scary.

"Deke, can I ask you a personal question?"

"You might as well," he said. "If I said no, you'd ask anyway."

I laughed. I grabbed a slice of pizza and handed it to him. "Why are you still a virgin? Aren't you ready to take your relationship with Yvonne to the next level?"

"No fair," Deke said, not looking at me. "That's two questions."

I thumped him on the side of his head. "Come on, tell me."

He took a bite of pizza, and chewed long and hard. His neck bulged as he finally swallowed. "I'm waiting," he said.

"For what? The right time of day? The right temperature?"

He laughed dryly. "Very funny. I'm waiting for the right girl, for the person I want to spend the rest of my life with."

"So you're waiting to get married?"

"To be honest, I don't know if I could wait that long. I'm just waiting to fall in love."

I scrunched my face up. "Love. That's the worst four-letter word in the dictionary. And I didn't think you cursed."

"Love isn't that bad."

"How do you know?" I demanded. "Are you in love with Yvonne?"

He laughed so hard, a piece of pepperoni flew out of his mouth and landed on my leg. "Sorry about that," he said as he picked the food off my leg and popped it back in his mouth. "I can safely say that Yvonne and I are not in love with each other."

"Y'all have been together for over a year." I said. "How do you know you're not in love?"

"I just do."

"Well…have you ever been in love before?"

Deke coughed. "Don't you think we're too young to fall in love?"

I arched my eyebrow. "That's a good question. I've never thought about it before. I've never *had* to think about it before."

"So you're saying you've never been in love," he said.

"I'd just as soon cut off my foot."

Deke rolled his eyes. "Not a pretty picture."

"You're telling me," I said. "Personally, I don't think I believe in love."

"How can you say that?"

"Love isn't all about frolicking in a field of daisies and serenading someone under the moonlight. Love is about self-sacrifice and crap like that. It just ain't for me."

"When did you become the authority on love?"

"When I found out my father was still alive." I waved a pizza crust at him. "If my parents were so much in love, as my mother claimed, why did he leave her?"

Deke's mouth gaped open. "I don't know."

"That's why love sucks."

"You sound kinda bitter."

I shrugged. "Just calling it like I see it."

There was silence as we finished the rest of the pizza. We usually didn't say much while we were eating. Deke was always too busy stuffing food into his mouth for idle chit-chat.

After he finished his fifth slice of pizza, he looked at me, but didn't say anything. I was waiting for him to ask for some of my food, like he usually did at about this time into a meal. But he remained quiet and continued to stare at me. Finally, he cleared his throat.

"Once," he whispered.

"Once? What are you talking about?"

"The answer to your question," he began as his gaze settled in his lap. "Have I ever been in love...."

I perked up and scooted closer to him. "You never told me that before."

"You never asked."

"Who is she?"

Deke's face scrunched up. "You're mighty nosy, aren't you?" He stood up. "I'm going for a walk."

"Cool," I said, slowly. I rose from the bed and grabbed my bag. "I'm going to take a shower."

I was kind of surprised at myself for letting Deke get away with his feeble attempt to dodge my question. But while I was dying to hear more about his mystery love, I knew he wouldn't discuss it until he was ready.

After sitting in the damp, sticky air for most of the day, it felt wonderful to take a shower. Luckily, the once brown water had become clear, clean, and hot. After more than my fair share of time, I forced myself to get out of the tub. I dried off, and threw on a pair of sweatpants and an oversized t-shirt. I wiped off the mirror and stared at myself. My father's side of the family must have consisted of light-skinned, flat-chested, gray-eyed black women.

"What took you so long?" Deke asked as I stepped out of the bathroom.

I winked at him. "Feminine issues. You wouldn't want to know."

"Y'all use that excuse for everything." He pushed past me into the bathroom.

I collapsed on my bed and began watching TV. The only decent thing on was a nature show. *The Life and Death of the Field Mouse.* They were just going into mating when Deke stepped out of the bathroom. His towel draped his shoulders and a pair of shorts hung at his waist. As he walked back into the room, his gaze fell on the TV.

"That mouse has more of a social life than I do," he said.

"You and me combined." I tried not to notice the few droplets of water that ran down his chest.

I felt another small ripple go through me. Were his shoulders always that broad?

Deke, sans shirt and shoes, kneeled at his bedside and folded his hands together. I assumed he was praying, but to whom I didn't know. It certainly couldn't be God. He was probably too busy playing poker with Santa Claus and the Tooth Fairy to hear Deke's prayers.

Deke opened his eyes and looked at me. "Is something wrong?"

It was then that I realized I was still staring at him. I could feel my face getting hot.

Deke laughed and slipped into his bed. "Who's the one blushing now?"

Deke and I walked out of the mechanic's garage. I stuffed the five one-hundred dollar bills into my pocket. "That's the last time I buy foreign."

"You're going to ruin any car when you don't fill it with radiator fluid and oil. You're lucky he paid as much as he did for that car."

"Maybe I can use this money for a down payment on a new one."

"Why don't you use it to buy a plane ticket so you can fly to Oklahoma, instead of trying to pull a stunt like this again?"

I opened the car door and stepped in. I had always loved riding in Deke's car. It smelled like a mix between a newly printed comic book and a burrito. The worn bucket seats conformed just the right way to my body. I yawned and nestled into position.

"Didn't get enough sleep last night?" he asked.

"No, I was too hot with all those clothes on."

He smiled. "You could have taken them off."

"You would have liked that, wouldn't you?" I strapped on my seat belt. "I'll be okay in a few minutes."

Truth of the matter was, I was worn out. I had fallen asleep easily enough, but I kept dreaming and waking up. The first dreams were about meeting my father. They weren't anything new; I had had them since learning he was alive. It was the last one that bothered me. It was about Deke. I couldn't remember much, but I did know he was selling beer at a Little League game, with nothing on but a pair of biker shorts and a cowboy hat.

Note to self: *Don't drink the water in Alabama.*

"Ready to go back?" Deke said as he buckled his seat belt.

"You know, I was thinking. Since we've come this far…"

"No."

"You don't even know what I was going to say."

"I can hear it in your voice. We are not going to Oklahoma. Your mother would kill me."

I smiled. "She can't kill you in Oklahoma."

He started the car and pulled into the street. "Even if I did want to go to Oklahoma, which I don't, I don't have any clothes to wear."

I pulled the wad of money out of my pocket and waved it under his nose. "You could always buy some."

He pushed the money out of his face. "We are not going to Oklahoma. Absolutely, positively, no way. And that's final!"

CHAPTER 4

"Why couldn't your father live in a town that was closer to the interstate?" Deke asked as we sped along a state highway.

"At least we don't have to go down any dirt roads." I looked at the cows grazing along the highway. "Not yet, anyway."

As Deke flew around a curve, I grabbed hold of the dashboard. "Maybe you should slow down."

"I'm only going twenty miles over the speed limit."

I picked up the two speeding tickets he had gotten earlier that day. "If they wanted you to go twenty miles above the limit, it would be set at eighty-five miles per hour, not sixty-five." I waved the tickets in his face. "You're going to kill yourself one day if you aren't careful."

"I'm not afraid of dying. Are you?"

The hairs began to rise on the back of my neck. "I know I don't want to die anytime soon."

"When I die, it will be after I have completed everything in this world God wants me to do."

My voice softened. "I don't like talking about death."

"There's nothing wrong with death. Everyone has to die at some point," he said. "Anyway, I don't have anything to worry about. When I die, I'm going to heaven."

"Is that what they call cemeteries nowadays?"

Deke rolled his eyes. "According to the map, we should reach town in about fifteen minutes." He glanced at me quickly, before focusing back on the road. "Are you nervous about meeting your father?"

I nodded. I was so nervous, my stomach felt like it was doing a trampoline act on my intestines. I was at the point where I had gnawed off most of my fingernails and was about to move on to my big toe.

"What do you think he'll be like?" I asked. "I hope he likes me."

"What's not to like?"

"Plenty," I said. "Half the time, *I* don't even like me."

Deke laughed, but I wasn't joking. There really was a lot that could go wrong. I didn't know if I could stand being disappointed.

I clutched Deke's arm. "Maybe we made a mistake. It's not too late to turn around."

"Turn around? I'd just as soon drive off a cliff."

"We could do that, too."

Deke sucked his teeth. "As soon as you meet him, you'll feel a lot better. You're just scared."

"I am not scared," I said. I puffed out my chest, as if it would make me feel more confident. "I just don't want to make an ass out of myself."

"You've been doing that for years. Don't stop now; you're getting good at it."

I dug what remained of my fingernails into his skin. "You know how to make a girl feel special, don't you?"

"Hey, that's what I'm here for," he said.

Slowly the landscape changed. As we approached the town, the amount of trees declined and the number of buildings grew.

Deke passed another speed limit sign, without slowing down. "After we settle in, remind me to call my parents again. They weren't in their hotel room when I called earlier and…." Deke's voice trailed off, and he looked at me out of the corner of his eye.

"Maxine, please tell me that you called your mother."

"Where did that come from?" I asked. I pointed to the speedometer. "You'd better slow down."

The car seemed to accelerate instead. "Don't try to change the subject."

"I wasn't trying—"

"Maxine…."

I sighed and folded my arms. "No, I didn't call her."

"Why not?"

"I didn't know what to say to her."

We rode a few more miles. "I knew you wouldn't call her," he said. "That's why I called her this morning when we stopped for breakfast."

I sat up. "Did you tell her we were driving to Oklahoma?"

Deke nodded. "She wasn't home or at work, so I ended up leaving a message on the answering machine."

I could imagine the grimace that must have been on Mom's face as she heard that message. As much as I hated deceiving her by driving to Oklahoma, this was something I had to do. I just hoped in the process of gaining a father, I didn't lose a mother.

I rolled down the window and stared at the landscape. It was just beginning to get dark. A group of kids played jump rope in one yard. A few houses down, an elderly couple sat on the porch, no doubt gossiping about the latest news.

"Do you see these houses?" I asked. "I feel like I'm looking at a Norman Rockwell painting."

Each house looked the same. All of them had enormous front lawns of newly mowed green grass, set off by gigantic, multicolored maple trees. I closed my eyes and took a deep breath. I could almost smell the freshly baked apple pies I imagined were sitting on every windowsill.

"So, which way do I turn to get to your father's house?" Deke asked.

"I don't know," I mumbled. "I kinda forgot to get his address."

"What?' Deke yelled. He slammed on the brakes. "Please tell me that he knows we're coming."

"Well…."

"Maxine!"

"Sorry," I said, looking away from Deke's glare. "It kinda slipped my mind."

"Slipped your mind?" He threw his hands in the air. "For all you know, he could be out of town."

"That's a possibility."

Deke continued driving. "So now what are we supposed to do?"

"Call him." I pointed out of the window. "There's a pay phone."

Deke pulled up to the phone booth. He muttered something under his breath, but I figured it wasn't anything I wanted to hear. I jumped out of the car and dropped a few coins in the machine. I didn't have to look up the number; I had committed it to memory the first night Mom gave it to me.

"Hello?"

"Jack, this is Maxine."

"Maxine? Where are you? Your mother and I are worried sick about you."

"You talked to Mom?"

"Listen, where are you?"

I pulled away from the phone booth and looked around. "At the corner of Main and Hershey."

"So, you *did* decide to drive out here?"

"Yeah," I said. "I hope you aren't mad."

I waited for a response, but all I heard was mumbling voices on the other end of the phone. Who was he talking to? His wife? His daughter?

A few seconds later, the mumbling stopped. "You know, I shouldn't be surprised," he said. "You're probably just like Kathy."

Kathy? Mom hated it when people called her Kathy.

"Just continue up Main Street for two blocks. Turn left on Jacobs and go to the end of the road. My house is the last one on the right. You can't miss it."

I replayed his directions in my head. "Okay, I'll see you in a few minutes." I began to hang up the phone, but stopped. "And Jack, thanks."

"For what?"

"For not yelling at me."

"I understand how you must feel," he said. "We'll talk about it once you get here."

I smiled and hung up the phone. I was still smiling when I got back into the car.

"What made you so happy?"

"Nothing. It's just that my father is a great guy."

"Great guys don't run out on their families."

"Deke, please don't start. I'm nervous enough, without you throwing in your snide comments."

I gave Deke the directions. Before I knew it, we were at the house. It was smaller than the other houses I'd seen on Main Street. The sun had set by now, but I could see that white paint was flaking off the shutters. The lawn was neat and trimmed, although the grass was a little taller than the grass in the other lawns. An old pick-up truck and a newer car sat in the driveway. No toys were in the yard.

"Are you ready?" Deke asked.

"As ready as I'm going to be."

The driveway seemed to stretch out forever as we made our way to the house. The entire world seemed to have stopped turning; the only thing I could hear was my own breathing. I reached up to ring the doorbell, but hesitated. Deke placed a hand on my shoulder. I smiled and pressed the buzzer.

I heard a set of footsteps draw closer. A few seconds later, a man opened the door and looked at me. He was thin, with a pair of worn overalls on and wavy red hair.

And he was white.

I was speechless. I just stared at the guy as he beamed at me. I shook my head. This had to be a mistake.

"Um, I'm sorry," I said. "I must have the wrong house." I looked at Deke. "We must have taken the wrong turn." I began backpedaling toward the car.

"Maxine?"

I stopped and held my breath. How did he know my name?

I slowly walked back to the door. This town was so small, word must have spread that I was coming, I rationalized.

The white man opened the screen and stepped onto the porch. His gaze darted repeatedly from me to the ground. His Adam's apple reminded me of a yo-yo, the way it bobbed up and down along his throat.

"Yeah, I'm Maxine," I said. "Maybe you could help me out. I'm looking for—"

"Maxine? Is that you?" a voice called from behind the guy. I frowned. Did everyone in town know who I was? And why did she sound like my mother?

The woman opened the screen and stood behind the guy. Unless my mother had an identical twin sister, Katherine Phillips had followed me to Oklahoma.

"Mom?"

She nodded and placed her hand on the man's shoulder. "Maxine, this is Jack Phillips. Your father."

Instantly, my stomach fell to the ground. I could almost feel it bouncing between my feet. I turned and looked at Deke. His eyes were as wide as two deluxe chocolate cookies.

I stared back at Mom and Jack. Black and white. Salt and pepper.

Jack took a timid step toward me. "Aren't you going to say anything?"

I ran my hand over my face and through my hair. I coughed a few times, trying to find my voice. My head suddenly felt heavy. I blinked at them, trying to focus on either one or the other. I felt like I was looking at them from the bottom of a pool of water. I wanted to move away, but my feet felt like they had been cast in concrete.

So, not being able to move and not being able to speak, I did the only thing a typical half-white, half-black, red-headed, flat-chested, gray-eyed teenage girl could do.

I passed out.

CHAPTER 5

I opened my eyes. As I sat up in bed, a cold, damp towel fell from my forehead into my lap.

Where was I?

I jumped up and almost fell, before catching the bedpost and steadying myself. It was an old wooden bedpost, with numerous scratches and marks from what looked like years of use. It was strong and sturdy though, and it was the only thing keeping me from busting my butt on the floor. I slowly let go of the post and headed to the door.

I was at the end of a long hallway. The other doors were either shut, or the rooms were pitch black. The only room with any light in it was at the other end of the house.

As I tiptoed down the hallway, I began to hear pieces of a conversation. The voices were soft at first but grew louder as I got closer to the room. By the time I reached the edge of the doorway, I could fully hear the conversation.

"Are you sure she's going to be okay?" a voice asked. It sounded like Mom.

"I work at a hospital, Kathy. All she did was faint. It's not like she had a heart attack or anything."

I didn't immediately recognize that voice. It must have been Jack.

"Don't patronize me, and don't call me Kathy," Mom said. "You should have known better than to let that girl drive all the way out here."

"Let her? It wasn't as if I was driving the car. She was in *your* care. It was *your* fault she drove out here."

"How dare you—"

"It's neither of your faults," another voice said. I smiled. It was always like Deke to try to make order out of chaos. "If anything, it's my fault. It was my car; I'm the one who drove her here."

"Knowing her, she probably talked you into it," Mom said. "I swear, that girl gives me so much damn grief sometimes…."

"She didn't talk me into anything, Ms. Phillips."

Jack laughed. "What do you and my daughter have going on, son? When I was your age, I didn't try to impress a girl by driving her halfway across the country. Maybe you should try flowers next time."

"Jack, please," Mom said.

"I'm going to check on Maxine," Deke said, raising his voice. He walked out of the room and almost ran into me.

"Shhh," I whispered as I placed my finger to my lips. I pointed back down the hallway. He nodded and followed me to the bedroom.

"You shouldn't be up," he said after we entered the room. "Here, let me help you back into bed." He grabbed my arm and tried to guide me onto the mattress.

I shook his hand off and sucked my teeth. "I can do it myself, thank you very much." I climbed into bed and yanked the covers over me.

"You don't have to bite my head off," he said. "I'm only trying to help."

"Well, don't."

He sighed. "You want me to leave?"

"Yes."

He turned and opened the door. I slapped myself on the forehead. The last thing I needed to do was ostracize the only person who didn't want to kill me.

"Deke, wait."

He stopped, with one foot out the doorway, the other in.

"Come back in," I said. "I didn't mean to snap at you."

He reentered the room and shut the door. "How do you feel?"

"A little light-headed, but I'll be okay."

He sat on the edge of the bed and placed his hand on my forehead. "You feel hot."

"Like I said before, I'll be fine." I struggled to sit up on the bed.

Deke placed a pillow behind my back. "You didn't expect him to be white, did you?" he asked.

"Not in my wildest dreams." I pulled a strand of hair in front of my eyes and stared at it. "I guess that explains why my hair is so screwed up, why my skin is so screwed up, why *I'm* so screwed up. I'm not white or black, just confused."

"Just because you're part white—"

"This changes everything. I've lived my entire life thinking I was black. In a matter of seconds, every idea I had about myself was destroyed." I slid back underneath the sheets and covered my face with a pillow. "And it doesn't help for Mom to be here."

"She was worried about you."

"Worried?" I felt the tears welling in my eyes. "Why didn't she tell me? Don't I have the right to know?"

"Maxine...."

By now the tears were spurting down my cheeks. "Please leave. I want to be alone right now."

He squeezed my hand and left the room. I wrapped my pale arms around my pillow, and cried myself to sleep.

"Good morning, sleepy head," Mom said as I made my way into the kitchen. It was almost noon. Deke sat at the table, reading the newspaper. Mom and Jack were focused on me.

"How do you feel, honey?" Jack asked.

I froze once I heard his voice. It sounded just like it did over the phone. The hard part was associating the white body with the voice.

"I'm okay," I said. As I slipped into a seat at the table, Deke looked over his paper and winked at me.

"You probably need to eat a good meal." Mom walked to the stove. "I made your favorite: French toast and bacon."

She fixed a plate and placed it before me. I took my fork and stabbed at the food. For some reason, it didn't look as good as it usually did. I placed a bite in my mouth. It didn't taste the same, either.

"Do you like it?" she asked.

I forced a smile and chewed harder on the toast. "The best I've ever had."

Mom walked back to the stove with a satisfied look on her face. Before I took another bite, my gaze caught Deke's. The grimace on his face said it all; he knew I hated the food.

"When did you get in, Mom?" I asked as I turned away from Deke.

"Yesterday afternoon. Once I found out where you were headed, I caught the first flight out."

"That explains how you beat us here," I said.

Jack cleared his throat and nodded at Deke.

As if on cue, Deke stood up. "I'm going to drive around town for a little bit. Maybe see some of the sights."

I dropped my fork. "I'll go with you."

"No, you'd better stay here," Jack said. "Deke will be back in a few hours."

"He could go from here to Texas and be back in a few hours," I said.

"Don't tempt me," Deke said. He left, leaving me, Jack, and Mom alone.

I frowned at the two of them. I felt as out of place as a red polka dot in a world full of plaid.

"Maxine, I know what you're thinking…" Jack began.

I rolled my eyes.

"Okay, maybe I don't know what you're thinking. Why don't you tell me what's on your mind."

I looked at Mom. "Why didn't you tell me he was white?"

She sat beside me and reached for my hand. "I was going to, in time."

"In time?" I jumped up from the table. "You had eighteen years. How much time did you need!"

"Young lady, watch your mouth," Jack said.

"Watch your own goddamn mouth."

"Maxine!" Mom yelled. "Sit down, now!"

I chuckled as I dropped back to my seat. "I've got a black mother who lies to me and a white father who is a deadbeat dad," I said. "This sounds like a really bad sitcom."

Mom ran her fingers through her hair. "You're only making this harder on everyone. Let me try to explain."

I crossed my arms. "I'm listening."

"When you were a baby, your father got into a little…trouble, and had to leave us. I took my anger out on you instead of him. I vowed never to tell you anything about him. I'm sorry."

"Why? What right did you have to do that to me?"

"It's not all her fault, Maxine. If I had been a better man in the first place, none of this would have happened."

"What do you mean by that? What did you do to make Mom hate you so much?"

Instead of answering my question, Jack turned to Mom. "I think we should tell her everything."

Mom nodded. "She's old enough."

The hairs on my neck began to rise. What deep, dark secrets lay buried in my father's past? What if it was something I didn't want to know?

"I met your mother almost twenty years ago," Jack said. "We were so young then. Didn't have a care in the world. Kathy was a student at New York University. I was—well, I don't quite know what I was at the time. After a whirlwind romance, we eloped. Not exactly the smartest thing to do."

"About a year later, you came along," Mom said. "Jack named you in honor of his mother."

"Is she still alive?" I asked. "Your mother."

Jack's eyes lit up, as if candles were burning behind his pupils. "Mom died of cancer when I was still a child." He reached out to me and lightly touched my hair. "You look a lot like her."

"And what about your father?"

Jack yanked his hand away from me, as if I had burned it. His gray eyes had lost the luster they had carried just a few moments earlier. "He died a long time ago, too."

Jack looked at Mom. While they didn't speak any words, I knew they were saying everything they needed to with their gaze.

"There's something you're not telling me, isn't there."

Jack finally turned back to me. "About my parents, no. They're dead, end of story." He nodded his head as if to confirm it to himself.

"Jack, tell me the truth. Why did you leave?"

Jack rubbed his hands together like he was freezing. His skin was pale and covered in sweat. "I had to leave because I was a fugitive from the law." He cleared his throat. "I had to go to prison."

I pushed my plate away.

"Are you okay?" Mom asked.

I looked into my plate and stared at my reflection. My image shimmered and shook like I was a ghost.

Okay, Maxine, you can handle this. This didn't mean he was a bad man, did it?

My mouth was sticky and my stomach felt like it was boiling. The aroma of the French toast and bacon wafted to my nose. But the smells didn't belong together; they didn't agree with my stomach.

"I had been on the run from the police for some time," he continued. "Of course, your mother knew nothing about this. It was a few days before your first birthday when they finally caught me."

I wanted to look at him, but I couldn't tear my gaze away from my plate. I forced myself to cough, just to fill the silence. "Why did you go to prison?" I asked as my voice cracked. I finally looked at him. "What did you do?"

"I committed manslaughter," Jack said, with frigid, distant eyes. "I killed my best friend."

My stomach lurched, and I covered my mouth with my hand. I jumped up and sped to the bathroom. I had just lifted the toilet seat when everything from that morning spewed out of me.

There went breakfast.

"Honey, are you all right?" Mom asked as she pounded on the bathroom door.

I tried to speak, but doubled over instead and threw up again.

And there went yesterday's dinner.

I knelt over the toilet for a few moments, scared to stand in case lunch came flying out as well. After a few moments, I pulled myself up to the sink and splashed water on my face.

Mom was still banging on the door. "Maxine, can I come in?"

I reached over and locked the door. "Leave me alone! Both of you!"

"I know you must feel confused and hurt right now," Jack said. "Let me and your mother take care of you."

Immediately, the image of Jack standing over a bloody body flashed into my mind. This time, I didn't have the chance to make it to the toilet. I vomited right in the sink.

I turned the faucet on and tried to clean up my mess. A few more knocks came at the door.

"Maxine, let us in," Jack said.

"No!" I yelled again. I backed into the corner and grabbed the closest thing I could find to a weapon—the plunger.

"Just leave me alone," I moaned. "I need time to think."

Mom sighed. "Okay, we won't try to come in. But how long do you plan on staying in there?"

I didn't answer, because I didn't know.

Finally, Mom spoke. "We'll be right in the kitchen if you need us."

I listened as their footsteps retreated down the hall. I leaned against the wall and slowly slid to the floor.

I thought about everything they had told me that morning. I tried to push the image of Jack killing another human being out of my head, but I couldn't ignore it. I didn't know anything about the situation, but every time I closed my eyes, I pictured him standing over a handsome, black teenage boy. The boy's body was covered in blood and his limbs were twisted as if he were a rag doll.

The boy looked like Deke.

After who knows how long, another knock came to the door. Two soft, short raps.

I grabbed my plunger again. "I said to leave me alone!"

"Maxine, it's me."

I pulled myself up from the floor. "Deke?"

"I'm alone, Maxine. Can I come in?"

I inched out of my corner. I turned the lock, and slowly pulled the door back.

Deke stood in the hallway, arms open. I took a step back and allowed him to squeeze into the bathroom.

"Lock the door," I said.

He did as I asked. "Now what?"

I felt my bottom lip quivering as I dropped the plunger. Before I knew it, I was in his arms, crying, sinking to the floor.

I wiped my nose with the back of my hand. I tried to laugh, but ended up choking on my tears. "Jack's a…"

"Shhh," he said, rocking me slowly in his embrace. "Don't worry about it now. Just cry."

So I sat there in my best friend's arms and cried until I couldn't cry any more.

CHAPTER 6

I don't know how Deke did it, but somehow he managed to get me out of that house without seeing either Jack or my mother. I didn't know where we were going, but I knew anywhere else was better than there.

After driving around Chickasha for a couple of hours, Deke and I pulled up to a small, dingy diner. Hundreds of insects hummed and buzzed around the light by the door. A number of large trucks were parked in the lot out front. Any minute now, I expected a guy with a hockey mask and a chainsaw to rush out of the woods.

"Do we have to stop here?"

"Nowhere else is open," Deke said. "It's either here or back to Jack's place."

My insides jumped. "I'll take my chances here."

We walked inside the diner. A couple of white men leaned against an old, dusty jukebox. One guy was younger, with a patch of black stubble on his chin. Tufts of greasy, black hair poked from under his faded cap. As he flashed me a smile, he almost looked proud to be missing his two front teeth. The older guy wore a matching cap. A cigarette dangled from his lips, the ashes barely clinging to the edge.

I rubbed at my skin. I guess these were my new "brothas."

I fell in step behind Deke and followed him to a booth. I picked up a menu. It felt as though it had been dipped in lard.

"Deke, why don't you let me pick up the bill?"

He shook his head. "You don't have to."

"I want to."

Before he had a chance to respond, the waitress ambled over to our booth. She was a black woman, the first I had seen in the town. She looked to be thirty-five going on seventy. Her face was covered with large moles that seemed to weigh her skin down. Thick blue veins climbed her brown legs. Her white apron was covered with stains from who knows what. She shifted her weight from one leg to the other and pulled a pencil and pad from her pocket.

She looked at Deke. "What do you want?"

"I'm not quite ready to order yet."

"Slowpoke," I muttered under my breath. He responded by kicking my leg under the table.

"Y'all just want to order drinks now?" she asked, still looking at him.

Hell no, I know what I want. Number one, I want a chicken sandwich. Number two, I want my father to be a normal guy, not a murderer. Number three, I don't want to be white.

Deke cleared his throat. "I'll take water."

"Me, too."

She stuffed the pad back into her pocket. "I'll be back in a few minutes for your order," she said to Deke, before she turned and left the booth.

Deke watched her walk off. "Are you sure you want to eat? Can your stomach handle it?"

"It'll be fine," I said. I nodded in the direction where the waitress had disappeared. "Did you hear her? She barely noticed I was breathing."

"What are you talking about?" His face was buried in his menu. "I wonder if the steak is any good?"

"Deke, stop thinking with your stomach for a few minutes." I reached over and pulled the menu from his face. "Didn't you notice what just happened? She talked to you like you were in charge, just because I'm a white girl."

"You're not white."

I wadded up a napkin and threw it at him. "Maybe you didn't notice the tall, red-headed white guy claiming to be my father."

"Your mother is black. That makes you black, too," he said. "You don't even look white."

"Are you sure about that?" I asked. "All of this time, I thought I was a really fair-skinned black girl." I shook my head. "It turns out I'm just a white girl with a good tan."

"Maxine...."

I turned from him and looked toward the counter. Our waitress slowly made her way back to our table. She placed the glasses in front of us and pulled her pad and pencil out again. As before, she directed the conversation toward Deke.

"Are y'all ready to order?"

"Yes, I think—"

"Yes, we're ready to order," I snapped, cutting Deke off.

The woman looked at me out of the corner of her eye. "What will you be having tonight?"

"I want a chicken sandwich, with fries. Extra mayo."

She looked back at Deke. "And what about you—"

"He'll be having the large T-bone. Well done, with a loaded baked potato."

Both Deke and the waitress looked at me like I was crazy.

Deke shook his head. "Um…"

"Okay, scratch that," I said, pressing my face to the menu. "Instead of the steak, he'll take the catfish, with sides of corn on the cob and mashed potatoes."

"What?" Deke said. "Listen, I—"

"Okay, he'll take both."

The waitress stopped writing. "Both?"

"Yeah, both." I nodded my head and crossed my arms. *Take that.*

Deke shrugged. "Fine with me."

She shot me a fleeting look. "Your dinner will be ready in a few minutes."

I could hardly contain my smile as the waitress walked off. "I showed her, didn't I?"

"Yeah, you showed her." Deke took a sip of water. "But for future reference, all I wanted was a hamburger."

"Well, you can take the extra food home with you."

"Speaking of which," he began, "you know you don't have to go back to Jack's house if you don't want to."

"I'm a big girl, I can handle it."

A big, white girl.

Deke ran his fingers across his mouth. His lips were full and red. His nose was broad and well defined. His black skin was like new, rich soil. One look at him and you couldn't think he was anything but black. I looked into the window. The glass and the dark night acted as a mirror. I noticed how thin and pink my lips were; how pointy my nose was. Now I knew why I had never seen any other black people with gray eyes.

"How do you feel?" he asked.

"White," I said.

"Okay, you're part white. So what?"

I frowned. "So what?" I said, before chuckling. "I'm a mutt. A half-breed. A chocolate-vanilla swirl."

"Don't you think you're overreacting?"

"And just how am I supposed to react?"

Deke didn't answer my question. As we sat in silence, I became more and more agitated—at what, I wasn't exactly sure. I was mad at Jack for not being the father I expected him to be. I was mad at Mom for lying to me.

I was mad at myself for believing in happy endings.

"Maxine?"

I snapped out of my trance. Our food sizzled in front of us. I hadn't even noticed the waitress had brought it to the table.

Deke had already begun attacking his food. I stared as he cut and stabbed and bit into his dark, juicy steak. It all reminded me of my father, and what he had done.

Deke paused. "Aren't you hungry?"

I picked up my plate and threw it to the floor. "What do you think?"

The waitress ran back over to the table. For a big woman, she sure could move fast. She planted her fists on her hips.

"Girl, what's wrong with you? You're paying for that plate."

"Okay, that's it." Deke stood up. "Let's go."

I frowned. "I'm not going—"

Before I knew it, Deke had picked me up and flung me over his shoulder. With his opposite hand, he dropped some bills on the table. Through red eyes, I watched the two men by the jukebox become smaller and smaller as Deke marched toward the door.

"Maxine, get a hold of yourself," he said. He dropped me on the ground in front of his car. "What's wrong with you?"

I tried to ignore the tears streaming down my face. "He murdered someone."

"He was only convicted of manslaughter."

I snarled and glared at him. "Are you taking up for him?"

Deke raised his hands as if he could block my gaze with them. "I'm only stating the facts."

By now, my shoulders were jerking uncontrollably. I curled into a ball, hoping that I could stop myself from shaking. "The facts are, I'm white, and my father's a killer."

Deke dropped to the ground and wrapped his arms around me. I clutched at his back, biting my lip to stop the sobs.

He pulled me up and brushed the dirt off my clothes. "Come on," he whispered.

I shook my head. "I can't go back there. Not tonight." I pulled some money out my pocket and pressed it into the palm of his hand.

He looked at the money in his hand, and nodded. "Okay, not tonight."

I followed Deke into the motel room. It was a small, shabby room, about as big as an airplane bathroom and just as unappealing. A tiny TV sat in the corner, with a beat up coat hanger antenna poking from its rear. I turned it on; the only thing I could see was gray static.

I stared at the TV as if the static was prime-time programming. Maybe staring at a fuzzy screen was better than staring at Deke. We hadn't spoken since leaving the diner. I couldn't even look at him. Every time I saw him, I was reminded of how black he was and how black I wasn't.

I finally turned off the TV and focused my attention on the bed. It looked barely twin-size, with a lone pillow jutting from underneath the blanket. Either the bed was made very hastily, or it was an extremely lumpy mattress.

I sat on it, and hung my head. "I don't know what's worse: being white, or being the daughter of a murderer."

"You're still the same Maxine that you were yesterday."

I looked at Deke and tried to focus on his eyes. They were the most non-black things about him.

"I must have seemed like a real fool out there in the diner parking lot."

"That was nothing compared to your performance in the bathroom with that plunger." He sat beside me on the bed. "I didn't know what you were doing with it."

"Me neither," I said. "Maybe I was trying to unclog the shitty mess that my life is."

"Your life is not a mess."

I rolled my eyes.

"It's not an easy life, but no one said that it would be easy," he began. "God—"

"Dammit, can't we have one conversation without you bringing up God?"

Deke cleared his throat. His jaw stiffened, before finally relaxing. "What do you have against God?"

"He tricked me," I said. "For years, I would close my eyes, kneel at my bed, and pray for a father. For a daddy to buy me ice cream and keep me safe from the imaginary monsters hiding in my closet." I laughed. "I even used to sit in my room and practice calling people

'Daddy,' so when Mom finally married someone, I wouldn't mess it up."

"But your mom never remarried," Deke said.

I nodded. "I finally wised up and stopped wasting my time with prayer and childish fantasies. But then I got the call and suddenly I had a father. And like a fool, I started to believe that maybe God had answered my prayers."

"You're not a fool."

"Whatever," I said. "God gave me a father, but not without a catch—not only is my father white, he's also a killer." I shrugged. "I guess I should have read the fine print at the bottom of my Bible."

"Maxine, you can't seriously blame God for—"

"He's all powerful, all mighty, isn't He?" I yelled. I got in Deke's face. "Isn't He?"

"Yes."

"Then why is He letting this happen to me?"

"I don't know."

I got up and walked around the room. I was able to take about three steps before I had to turn around and head the other way. "You're always the one preaching about the consequences of sinning," I said. "What sin did I commit to deserve this life?"

"I don't know."

"You know, you say that a lot." I pulled the nightstand drawer open. Sure enough, a Bible lay inside it.

"Why don't you try looking in here?" I flung the book at him. "That has all the answers, doesn't it?"

Deke clutched the Bible like it was his most prized possession. "I don't believe this," he said, "but hypothetically, let's say God is out to get you. What are you gonna do about it?"

I turned the TV back on as if the answer to all my problems lay encoded in the static. "I wish I knew."

CHAPTER 7

There was number eighteen buying a newspaper. Deke and I drove by numbers nineteen and twenty as they stood on the corner having a conversation. Number twenty-one drove by in the opposite direction, singing along to whatever song was playing in the car.

We were almost at Jack's house before I realized what I was doing. I was counting men. Brothers, fathers, sons. Some were going to work; some had no intention of doing anything close to resembling work. Some were taking their sons and daughters to camp, or to the zoo, or wherever. No doubt some had children they refused to take anywhere.

As Deke pulled into the yard, I focused on number twenty-two, Jack Phillips. A man I didn't know. A man I would probably never see again. A man that was, better or worse, my father.

"I don't know anything about him," I mumbled. "I don't even know when his birthday is."

Deke frowned. "Maxine, are you okay? Are you sure you're ready to see him again?"

"I'm fine," I said. "I just had to get my thoughts together. I have an important announcement for my parents."

"What...that you want to leave?"

"No," I replied. "That I want to stay."

"What?"

I looked at Mom. "I want to stay."

Mom and Jack stared at me like they didn't understand what I said. *What, did I stutter?*

"Maxine, I don't think now is the best time for you to visit," Jack said. "Maybe you could come back in a few months, when you're ready."

"I know if I leave now, I'll never come back," I said as I crossed my arms. "I'm not going anywhere, at least not for a few days."

"And just how long is a few days?" Mom asked.

"A week. A week and a half."

Deke sat on the couch beside me. "Just yesterday, you were ready to disown both of them. Now, you want to stay here, with *him*?" He leaned closer to me. "Are you sure you want to do this, after what you know about him?"

"A week won't kill me."

Deke frowned. "You don't know that." He shook his head and stood up. "Your daughter is crazy," he muttered as he pushed past Jack and left the room.

Jack sat down in the spot Deke had vacated. I tried to stop myself from flinching as his bare arm grazed mine. "I'd love for you to stay," he said. "But maybe you'd better talk to your mother about this first."

I waited until Jack left the room. "Well, can I stay?"

Mom chewed on her lip long and hard before speaking. "I can't believe I'm saying this, but you can stay—if it's okay with Jack, and only for a week."

I was hugging her before she finished her sentence.

"You deserve the chance to get to know him," she continued. "I took that right away from you before. I won't do it again."

"Thanks," I whispered into her neck.

"But don't think that you're not in trouble. The second you get home, you're grounded. And you can forget about a new car to replace the old one. No car, no phone, no internet, no life."

I was so happy I could stay, Mom could have taken away anything she pleased. I was staying, and that was all I wanted.

Mom pulled away from me. "I'll change my plane reservations for next week. I have a few sick days, and I'm sure someone at the office can cover for me."

My mouth dropped open. Was Mom taking vacation, for me? Why couldn't this have happened when I wanted to go to Disneyland?

I grabbed her hand and squeezed it. "Mom, you can't stay."

"It's no problem, Maxine. They'll understand at work."

I shook my head. "No, you don't understand. I don't want you to stay."

"Oh, I see."

I sighed and wrapped my arm around her. "Don't get the wrong idea. I'm not angry with you."

She rolled her eyes.

"Well, I am a little angry. But, I kinda see why you did what you did."

"Won't you feel uncomfortable staying here with Jack, without me around?"

"Probably. But if I'm going to have any type of relationship with my father, it has to come about without you breathing down my neck."

Slowly, she nodded her head. "I…understand. But I'm going to ask Deke to stay with you."

"What? What's Deke going to do around here?"

"Help keep you out of trouble. I trust Deke, and I know he'll be there for you if you need him." She rose and walked to the door. "You probably don't even see how he feels about you."

"Of course I do. He's my best friend."

"And the doctor said you didn't need glasses," she said before she left the room.

I slipped into my seat and tried not to drool on the table. My eyes showed me what my nose had already detected. I had first smelled the fried chicken from the end of the hallway. Beside the chicken sat a bowl of mashed potatoes.

I unfolded my napkin and laid it in my lap, just as Mrs. Webster had shown us in etiquette class. I flashed a small smile at the others. Mom sat beside me and Deke sat across from me. Jack sat at the head of the table. I guess that was where the father was supposed to sit.

"I'm starving," I said as I reached for the basket of bread. "Did you cook all of this, Jack?"

"No, one of the ladies from church brought it over."

"How did they know to cook so much?" Deke asked.

"Word travels fast around here," Jack said. "Most everyone in the church knows that y'all are in town."

"It's hard to miss us," I mumbled.

Suddenly, I felt a sharp pain in my leg. I looked up at Deke. He glared at me before passing the food.

I picked up my fork and dug into my potatoes. After its long absence, my appetite had finally returned. With my bony figure, I couldn't afford to lose one meal, much less three. My chest could use all the help it could get. I brought my fork to my mouth and blew on it. The potatoes were still steaming.

"Maxine, before we eat, we need to bless the food," Jack said.

"I don't do that anymore," I said, before placing my fork in my mouth.

"Maxine," Mom said, "could you show your father a little courtesy?"

"What do you mean, you don't do that anymore?" Jack asked, frowning. "Are you an atheist?"

"No, I'm not an atheist," I said. "I believe there is a God. I just choose not to pray to Him."

Jack looked at Mom as if he had been slapped. "Is this true?"

Mom shrugged. "You know I was always one to let people choose their own destiny."

"Oh, you won't let her come and visit her own father, but you let her be a…devil worshiper?"

"I'm not a devil worshiper. I just kill small rodents for fun," I said. "You know, dead rats look beautiful in the moonlight."

Jack slammed his hand on the table. "Enough!" He glared at every-one, before stopping on me. "I'm going to bless the food. And while you're in my house, you're going to bless the food also." He folded his hands in front of him. "Please bow your heads."

"But—"

"Bow your head," he said again.

I rolled my eyes and did as he said. While he prayed, I revamped my Shit List. It was full of people who really pissed me off. I mentally wrote his name on the sheet of paper, right under God's.

I opened my eyes once I heard the clink and clatter of silverware. Finally. I picked up my fork and began eating.

Jack cleared his throat. "So, Deke, I hear you're going to Howard University in the fall. What are you majoring in?"

Deke didn't look up from his food. "Computer Science."

"I see." He eyed me, before looking back at Deke. "How long have you known Maxine?"

"Since kindergarten," Deke said, with his face still in his plate.

"That's a long time," Jack said.

Deke grunted a reply.

Jack sighed. "Well, do you believe in God?"

Deke finally looked up. "Yes sir. Very much so. I love the Lord."

"Let's be honest," Jack said as he put his fork down. "Are you hav-ing sex with my daughter?"

I was so surprised, I dropped my fork, loaded with mashed pota-toes, in my lap. "What? Are you serious?"

Jack continued to glare at Deke. "Well, son?"

The expression on Deke's face reminded me of how I felt about Algebra: hopelessly confused. "Of course I'm not sleeping with her," he finally said.

"Are you sure?" Jack said. "I see the way you look at her."

"Jack, what's wrong with you?" Mom asked. "Of course he's sure."

I sighed. "Obviously Jack is too smart for us to trick him." I turned to Jack. "Yes, Deke and I are sleeping together. Twice a night, three times on Sundays."

"That wasn't funny," Jack said.

"Who was being funny?" I said. "Sometimes, Mom takes pictures."

Jack grimaced. "Call me old fashioned, but I don't like the idea of someone lusting for my daughter while sleeping under my roof. You never know what could happen." He broke off a piece of bread and stuffed it in his mouth.

We ate the rest of our dinner in silence. As soon as Deke and I were finished, I whisked him out of the kitchen and onto the porch. A wooden, rustic swing rocked in the wind. As we sat on it and began to sway, I began to feel more at ease.

"I'm sorry about Jack back there," I said.

Deke shrugged. "I'm cool."

I tried to ignore the iciness in his voice. "Did Mom talk to you yet?"

He nodded. "She wants me to stay, to keep an eye on you."

"How does your mom feel about that?"

"You know how she is," he said. "As long as I bring back a rock, it's okay with her."

Most people had interesting hobbies. They collected stamps or postcards, or things like that. Deke's mother collected rocks. She had a huge collection of assorted stones and pebbles, each from a different part of the world. I think the only reason she went to Hawaii was to bring back a rock.

And people said *I* was weird.

I pushed against the railing with my feet to make the swing sway faster. "What are you going to do?"

"I don't know."

"What's the problem? If you want to stay, then stay. If not, then go." I turned away from him and looked out across the field.

"You know what the problem is."

I listened to the wind whistle through the wooden planks of the porch. "You don't care for Jack much, do you?"

Deke stomped his foot on the ground and stopped the swing's gentle sway. "He abandoned you."

"Just because you can't forgive your father—"

"This isn't about me and my father. My father is in Hawaii with my mother."

I sighed. "Your *stepfather* is in Hawaii."

Deke pressed his lips together and formed a small grimace. "Jason Ashland is the only father I've ever needed."

"Don't you ever want to see your biological father again?"

"No."

"What about forgive and forget?"

Deke raised his foot and the swing began to move again. "I've forgiven my biological father, and now I choose to forget him."

Deke was eight when his father left home. At eight, Deke was as strong and as fast as the fifth and sixth graders. He would spend every possible moment playing football. And when he wasn't playing football, he was talking football. He could spit out football statistics like people breathed air. His father had been a professional player, and Deke spent every moment daydreaming of playing pro football like his father.

But one day, he stopped. No more football talk, no more football games. He even refused to play during gym class. It was many years later that Deke told me he stopped playing the day his father left.

I crossed my arms. "I understand how you feel, but I have to give Jack a chance."

"Why?" he asked. "You've lived eighteen happy years without a father. Why start now?"

"Happy? What makes you think my childhood was happy?" I said. "Do you know how jealous of you I am? You have parents that are always there for you. Now that I think about it, I spend more time with your parents than I do with mine. You have a mother who stays at home and cooks dinner every night. I've lived off hamburgers and microwave meals for most of my life." I shook my head. "You don't want to know how many times I've wished I was you."

Deke frowned. "I'm…sorry for what happened to you while you were growing up. But honestly, is staying here with your father the answer to your problems?"

"I don't know," I replied. "But he's my father. There are some things a daughter is supposed to do."

"Even if it means getting hurt?"

"I won't get hurt."

Deke snorted. "Maybe I shouldn't stay. I probably wouldn't be much help."

I thought about staying in Oklahoma without Deke. At first, I hated the idea of Mom asking him to stay. But hearing him say that he might leave made me feel a little scared.

"What do you want me to do?" he asked.

"What does Yvonne want you to do?"

"Don't answer a question with a question," he said. "And besides, Yvonne doesn't have anything to do with this."

I rolled my eyes. "I don't care. Do what you want."

He sighed. "It never changes with you, does it?"

"What are you talking about?"

"About you and your relationships with people. You tend to push away everyone who is close to you. Why?"

"I don't push people away. I'm just not a people person." I fanned at myself. "It's as hot here as it was in Alabama. Not as humid, though."

"Stop changing the subject."

"Make me." I stuck my tongue out at him.

"You and those snide comments." He stood up. "For your benefit, and your mother's sanity, I'll stick around. But you should know that I do not approve of this." He walked to the edge of the porch. "Whenever you want to leave, all you have to do is say the word."

I nodded. "Where are you going?"

"I feel like taking a walk. You want to come along?"

I declined, and watched him walk off into the sunlight. If it weren't for the black skin, I'd swear he was one of those heroes who walked off into the sunset at the end of a western movie. Deke Ashland, my black cowboy.

After a few moments of solitude, I rose from the swing and entered the house. I peeled my shirt from my back and waved my arms under the vent. Cold air blew down on my head. Who needed God when you had air conditioning?

I walked through the den but stopped at the doorway. I heard Mom and Jack's voices in the kitchen.

"I just don't like him," Jack said. "I thought his eyes were going to pop out of his sockets, the way he ogled at her."

"You're like any typical father. You don't like any boys Maxine's age," Mom said. "Deke's good for Maxine. He cares for her, like a true friend should. And he's very spiritual. He's as close to church as Maxine gets."

"How did she become so anti-religious?" Jack asked. "Do you think it was because I wasn't there?"

I leaned against the wall and sank to the floor. I knew I shouldn't be eavesdropping, but I couldn't help it.

"I don't know why she turned away from God," Mom said. "It's probably just a phase. She'll grow out of it."

Guess again.

"Maybe I can help her," Jack said.

"She's a little stubborn."

"So I've noticed." Jack laughed. "She's a lot like you."

"No, she's more like you," Mom said. "Every year, she reminds me more and more of you." There was a lull in the conversation. "You look good, Jack."

"So do you," he said, quietly. "I never thought I'd see you again."

"And me you," she said. "I see you've been taking care of yourself."

"Yeah, I've tried. There's nothing like fifteen years in the penitentiary to toughen you up."

"I thought about you, sometimes," she said.

There was more silence.

"Me, too," he finally replied. "Sometimes, the only thing that kept me from going insane in there was my faith, and the thought of you and Maxine."

"I wish things could have been different," she said. "I wish…"

"Shhh," he said. "It's all in the past now. Let's leave it there."

I listened as chairs scraped against the kitchen floor. The lights in the kitchen went dark, and footsteps faded down the hallway.

I had always wondered why my mother never remarried. She dated often enough, but things never seemed to materialize into anything more. There were a few guys who lasted longer, like Robert Salim. He was Muslim, so for the entire time he and Mom dated, we didn't eat pork. I don't know how may times I woke up in the middle of the night yearning for a thick, greasy, fried pork chop sandwich. I liked Robert and I thought Mom did, too. But I guess they didn't like each other enough, because they broke up after a year.

The way men gawked at her, Mom could have had almost any man in Columbia, or all of South Carolina for that matter. But she very rarely dated, and I think I always resented her for that, a little. I abhorred the idea of her marrying someone for my benefit, but I really did like it when there was a guy around the house like Robert always was. He was almost like a father, or the closest I could get to one.

I peeked into the kitchen and down the hallway. It was dark and deserted. I walked past Mom's room but stopped when something caught my ear. I couldn't tell if it was talking, or laughing, or what. I pressed my ear against the door.

It was crying.

As I stood in the hallway, ear against the door, I realized why Mom had never married Robert, or any other man.

She was still in love with Jack.

CHAPTER 8

"Good morning, sweetie," Mom said as she entered my room. Today was her last day here; her flight would leave this morning.

"Are you all packed?" I asked as I sat up and wiped my eyes.

She nodded, and sat on the bed.

"I was thinking, if you don't want to leave…"

"No, I think it's best that I go home," she said, before sighing deeply. "Thank you for offering though."

She brushed the hair back on my head. It reminded me of when I was a child, when I would wake up to her stroking my hair.

"You look so much like him," she said. "You're not as pale, but you have the same nose, the same mouth." She placed her hand on mine. "I'm sorry for not telling you earlier."

I shrugged. "If I were you, I probably would have done the same thing."

"No you wouldn't have," she said. "You've always been strong. You wouldn't have been afraid to tell your daughter the truth."

I leaned over and pecked Mom on the cheek. "You were just trying to protect me."

"Maybe. But I think I was a little selfish, too. I was so mad at him, of the situation he put us in." Her hand slightly squeezed mine. "I wanted to hate him, but I couldn't. Not then, not now."

"Mom, please stay. There's still a chance you and he could—"

She chuckled. "No, Maxine, I don't think so. Seeing him again just reaffirms what I've known for years."

"That you love him?"

"No, that I love what we could have been, but what we'll never be. There are just too many wrongs between us to make it right." She pulled her hand away from mine and walked to the door.

"Mom, wait," I whispered, so softly that I wasn't sure if she heard me at first. But she stopped and looked at me.

"I just want you to know…I'm not trying to replace you. I just need to know him."

Mom smiled. "I know, sweetie. When you get back home, I'll love you even more than I did when you left. You'll still be on punishment, but I'll still love you." She cleared her throat and glanced at her watch. "Now, hurry up and get ready," she said. "My flight leaves in three hours, and I have to take the car back to the rental agency."

I waved as Mom pulled into the street and drove off. She was supposed to have left thirty minutes ago, but she kept finding things to delay her. Finally, after squeezing ten years out of my life with her bear hug, we forced her into the rental car. I stood on the porch and watched as she faded into the horizon.

Jack clapped his hands together. "Are y'all ready to go?"

I frowned and looked at Deke. He looked back blankly at me. "To where?" I asked.

"To church."

Deke and I followed Jack's pick-up truck into the parking lot. I looked at the church. It wasn't the smallest church I had ever seen, but it was close. I figured a good twelve, thirteen people could fit inside, if they didn't breathe too hard. The red brick walls were old and chipped, but clean. A wooden steeple stood on top of the roof. A dented, bronze bell hung in the tower.

It had been three years since I had been inside a church. It had been a cold Sunday, much colder than Columbia usually got. I remembered carrying my little white Bible. It was a gift from my mother.

That morning, Pastor Jones came to the alter as he did every Sunday. He was a large man with calm, steady eyes and a deep, billowing voice. I wasn't sure, but it seemed as if he was staring at me, talking to me. He opened his mouth and eloquent words flowed from him. Words of prayer and sacrifice, and of God providing for our needs. I can still remember the verse in the Bible he quoted. It was the verse I had always found solace in, that kept me praying.

Matthew, Chapter 21, Verse 22: *And All Things, whatsoever ye shall ask in prayer, believing, ye shall receive.*

But that Sunday, I couldn't take it anymore. I couldn't sit there and listen to any more hollow promises. I walked out of the church, in the middle of the sermon, leaving my Bible in my seat. I never went back for it.

Deke and I followed Jack through the hallway and into an office. A teenage girl sat behind the desk.

"Abby, I'd like you to meet Maxine and Deke." He waved his arm in our direction.

Abby rose and extended her hand to me. As she stood, her perfect chest jiggled in front of us. "Hi, how are you doing?" she asked, in the worst country twang I had ever heard. She shook my hand and then looked at Deke. A sly smile spread across her face as she tucked her sun-bleached blonde hair behind her ear. "Welcome to First United Baptist Church."

Deke smiled and shook her hand. "It's nice to be here."

Wait a minute. I didn't like the way she was looking at Deke. And I definitely didn't like the way he was looking back.

"Abby, where is Mrs. Jackson?" Jack asked.

She nodded toward the window. "Outside, with the kids."

I stared at her skin. She looked as bronze as the bell on top of the church. And those teeth—they looked like someone painted them white.

"Are y'all going to be helping out with Vacation Bible School?" she asked.

I shook my head. "I think we're just here to meet someone." I looked at Jack. "Right?"

"Not exactly," he said. "I thought it would be good for you two to get out of the house." He placed his hand on my shoulder. "Anyway, I had to come out here to get some work done. I figured this would give us a chance to spend a little time together."

I shook his hand off my shoulder. "We can spend time together at home."

He sighed. "Abby, could you ask Mrs. Jackson to step in here?"

"Yes, sir."

I watched Deke stare at her as she left. Was that a smile on his face?

"Maxine, I'd appreciate it if you wouldn't cause a scene in front of people," Jack said.

I ignored his comment. "Is this some type of trick to get me to accept your religion?" I asked. "If it is, you may as well stop now. You're wasting your time."

"It's only Vacation Bible School," Jack said.

"Vacation Bible School?" I put my hands on my hips. "I don't even know what Vacation Bible School is."

"Look, the church needs students to help watch over the kids during activities. They also need students to help with lunch and snacks. It's not like you'd be preaching from a mountain top, for heaven's sake." He looked at Deke. "Deke doesn't mind doing it. Do you, Deke?"

Deke stared at us with his mouth gaped open. "Um..."

"Deke does mind," I said. "He's just too nice to complain. Isn't that right Deke?"

"Well, actually—"

"Anyway, it doesn't matter what he thinks. We don't want to do it. And we're not going to." I folded my arms and stared at Jack. "Ain't that right, Deke?"

I flipped the hair out of my face and dropped a frankfurter in a bun. "You're supposed to be on my side, Deke."

He shrugged and handed me another bun. "What did you want me to do, lie?"

"That would have been nice."

"Maxine, you're overreacting. There's nothing wrong with helping out at the church for a few hours."

Abby nudged my arm. "Really, it's not as bad as it looks. There isn't anything else to do in this poor excuse for a town, anyway." She looked at Deke. "Have you met anyone else in town yet, Deke?"

"No, *we* haven't," I said, glaring at her. "We just got here the other day."

Her smile grew larger. I didn't think that many teeth could fit in one person's mouth.

"I'm having a little get together at my place at about six," she said to Deke. "You're welcome to come if you want to." She nodded at me. "And of course, you can come, too."

There's no way we're going to your party.

"Sure," Deke said. "It sounds like fun."

I'd rather gouge my eyes out.

"You want to go, Maxine?" he asked.

"Sure, honey," I said in drawn out country drawl. I made three syllables sound like eight.

I moved away from Deke and Abby. The last of the children had been served and I'd be happy if I never saw another hot dog in my life.

What I really wanted to do was find Jack and apologize. I gagged as I thought about forcing an apology. It wasn't the easiest thing for me to do, especially when I didn't think I was entirely to blame. But if I was committed to making this relationship work with Jack, I had to at least try.

I walked out of the dining hall and into a hallway. Pictures of old white men hung from the walls.

I peeked in the office. Jack was sitting behind the desk, staring at a stack of papers. He looked up as I walked in the room.

"We've finished feeding the kids," I said. I slid into one of the chairs in front of the desk. "About earlier today, I'm sorry...."

He took off his glasses and placed them on top of his paperwork. "I should be the one apologizing. I should have told you about Vacation Bible School before I dragged you out here."

"I still shouldn't have been so defiant." I forced a smiled. "If I remember correctly, I'm sure the Bible says something about obeying your parents."

Jack stood. "Maxine, can we go for a walk? It tends to get a little stuffy in here."

I nodded and followed Jack out of the office. We remained silent as we walked outside and behind the church.

I could hear laughter from the children inside the building. All the little white children at ease playing their games. They didn't worry about living in the worst part of a city, going to sub par high schools, or struggling to get accepted to a college. They didn't have to worry about getting stopped by the police because they happened to be too dark to drive a nice car. Or they didn't have to concern themselves with salespeople in department stores following them around, thinking they were trying to steal the newest pair of two-hundred dollar sneakers. They could just grow up.

The path opened up to a garden. Red roses seemed to hang from every direction. Some were tightly closed as if they were afraid to let anyone see them. Others were in full bloom, proud of their beauty.

"What do you think?" he asked. His voice seemed to resound off the trees.

"It's beautiful." I took a deep breath, and tried to capture the scent of every rose. "With all of these trees, no one would ever know this is back here."

"I know. I like to come out here from time to time, when I need to think." He sat on a tree stump. "Why don't you pray anymore?" he asked.

"I just don't, okay." I picked a rose from a bush. "How long have these things been growing out here?"

"For at least two years."

"Is that how long you've been here?" I asked.

He nodded as he picked up a blade of grass and twirled it between his fingers. "Do you think God wronged you?"

"What's with all the questions about God?" I asked. "I'm sure He doesn't spend as much time thinking about us."

"How do you know?"

"How do you not know?" I plopped down on the ground, rose still in hand. I was careful not to prick myself. "What has God done for us?"

"He gave us life."

I shook my head. "I don't understand why God would allow us to live in such a messed up world. He gives us life, but He makes it seem like hell. You would think that He hates us."

"He doesn't hate us."

"He hates me."

Jack frowned. "Why do you think that?"

"I asked and asked for a father. I finally get one, years after the fact, and I find out he's...not quite what I expected."

"Not what you expected...?"

"I'm sorry, I didn't mean it like that. I—"

"It's okay," he said. "I know you were blindsided by this whole deal." Jack's gaze fell to the ground. "I know I'm not what you were looking for."

I searched for words to say, but couldn't come up with anything. I kicked off my shoes. My toes looked too skinny and too pink. I stuck them into the earth and felt the cool, black soil ooze between them.

"Tell me something about you," I finally said.

"What do you want to know?"

"You work at the hospital, right? What are you, a doctor or something?"

"I'm an orderly there. I do everything the doctors and nurses don't want or don't have time to do. I would be at work now, except I took the rest of the week off." He placed his hands behind his head. "Anything else you want to know?"

I stared at him for a second, and then looked away. "Was it a man or woman?"

He frowned at me.

"Your best friend. The person…"

"His name was Raymond," Jack said. "I had known him forever. Both of our fathers were preachers in our hometowns."

Maybe it was because I had a name to associate with his murdered friend, but all of a sudden, I felt my body go numb. "Tell me what happened," I whispered.

He walked from the stump and sat beside me. He was built a lot like me. He was tall and lanky, with shoulders that seemed to jut from his body. "Are you sure you want to hear this?"

I nodded. "I think so."

"Well it was a long time ago. I was a little older than you, still in seminary."

"Seminary?" I asked. "You wanted to be a minister?"

"Yes, a long time ago." His eyes seemed to sink into his face. "One night, while home from school, Ray and I went out to shoot some pool. The later the evening got, the more we drank, and the looser our lips became."

I frowned. "I didn't think preachers were supposed to drink."

"Preachers aren't supposed to do a lot of things," Jack replied. He closed his eyes before continuing his story. "Finally, after hours of drinking, Ray slipped and said something about my mother…I can't even remember what it was. But it was right after Momma had died…he said it, and I snapped. I know he didn't mean it. Ray was too juiced up to know what he was saying. But I was too juiced up to think rationally. How dare he insult Momma like that, I remember thinking to myself. So, with a spirit filled with rage, I lunged at him and unleashed all of my anger on him."

Jack sighed the saddest sigh I had ever heard. "When I opened my eyes, he lay at my feet. Dead."

He began to talk slower, in a deeper voice. "Once I realized what I had done, I panicked. I ran as far and as fast as I could. That's how I ended up in New York."

Jack looked like he was on another planet. A bee flew in front of his face, but he made no motion to shoo it away. His knees were drawn up to his body like he was a small child. He almost looked innocent, until the image of him standing over a body flashed in my mind. A man lay at his feet, his skull completely cracked open. His eyes were wide and full of terror. His skin was black.

"What color was he?"

"White." The bee continued to fly in his face. "Back then, around here, black and white folks weren't very friendly with each other."

I scowled. "That didn't stop you and Mom."

"Things were different in New York. People were more understanding." He finally noticed the bee buzzing around him and swatted it away. "Don't get me wrong, we still got plenty of dirty looks. Every so often, we'd get some hate mail," he said. "You know, people can be really ignorant. They don't understand that love has no color boundaries."

I rolled my eyes. "That sounds like something a white person would say."

"What do you want me to do, apologize for being white?"

"That's a start."

"I can't do that," Jack said. "It's unfortunate that you don't approve of me being white, but there's nothing I can do about it."

"Why didn't you tell me over the phone?"

"I didn't think about it," he said. "I don't go around thinking about my skin color every day."

"You're white; you can do that," I said. "But there's not a day I don't get reminded I'm black, not a day I don't have to deal with it."

I stared at my pink toes before stuffing them back into my shoes. "But thanks to you, I don't have to worry about being black anymore, do I?"

CHAPTER 9

Deke stopped at the intersection before turning. "I saw you sneak off with your father earlier this afternoon. I assume y'all had a chance to talk."

"Yeah, something like that." I looked at my watch. "Are we almost there?"

"Don't be so impatient." He slowed and pointed. "I think that's the house," he said as he pulled up to the curb. "Just don't make a scene, please."

"Who, me?"

He turned off the car. "No, the other psychopath with the cherry-brown hair."

A row of cars lined the driveway and the curb in front of the house. It was a huge house, with at least three stories. It was made of excessively bright red bricks, which looked as if they had just been dipped in nail polish. Tall evergreen trees lined the edges of the property, acting as a natural fence to all those not welcome.

A group of people, about our age, talked together on the front lawn. Most everyone was in swimwear, flaunting their perfect bodies. It seemed like every guy's stomach was flat and every girl's chest was perky. I looked down at my chest. I had my bathing suit on, but it was safely hidden underneath a t-shirt and pair of jeans.

I spotted Abby as we stepped out of the car. She ran up, bouncing all the way, and threw her arms around Deke. He looked surprised as he wrapped his arms around her and returned the embrace. I didn't care what Deke said about not making a scene. If she tried to hug me, I'd punch her.

She wore a blue bathing suit that accentuated every curve she had. She smelled of chlorine and barbecue. Her hair was pulled back in a ponytail with water still dripping from the end.

I patted my own hair. I hadn't even tried to do anything with it. I usually had to manhandle it just to get it to lie how I wanted. If I had tried to put it in a ponytail, I would still be at home, fighting with it.

"Come on," she said, already pulling Deke behind her. "Let me introduce you to everyone."

Reluctantly, I followed Abby and Deke into a crowd of teenagers. In five minutes, I met more Bobs, Johns, Sues and Jennies than I had ever met before. Naturally, they were all white.

I smiled and shook everyone's hand as Abby whisked us past each person. Finally, she stopped at a group of students. In the middle of them stood a black guy.

I stopped and wiped my eyes. Black folks, here? I snorted. Knowing my luck, he'd end up being the butler.

"This is Marcus," she said, pointing to the guy. He was a few inches taller than Deke, but thinner. I could see the outline of his pectorals through his muscle shirt. His arms looked like he had grown up chopping wood. His onyx-like skin glistened in the sunlight. Just looking at him intoxicated me.

I have *got* to move to Oklahoma.

"Marcus is the star basketball player at our high school. Probably one of the top prospects in the state," Abby said, beaming at him. "He's also an honor student."

"And who are you?" he crooned.

I just stared at him, soaking in his voice. It was sex for the ears.

Deke elbowed me. "Her name is—"

"Maxine," I blurted out, finally realizing Marcus was talking to me. I quickly reached out and shook his hand. It was strong and warm to the touch.

"I don't remember seeing you in town before," he said. He continued to hold my hand. "Are you new here?"

"Maxine is Deacon Phillips's daughter."

Marcus's eyes widened as he looked at Abby.

Great, I've just met him, and I'm already tainted goods.

To my surprise, he turned back to me and smiled. "Welcome to Chickasha." He leaned closer to me. "Is what they say about church girls being wild true?"

Abby slapped him on the arm. "She just got here, Marcus. You can at least let her get something to eat before you start hitting on her."

He winked at me, before finally letting go of my hand. "Find me later on," he said, before walking off.

I watched as his tight butt moved away from me. *Left cheek, right cheek, left cheek, right—*

"Maxine?" Deke said as he waved his hand in front of my face. "Did you hear me?"

I didn't break my gaze from Marcus's butt. "Every word."

Deke sighed, and I finally turned my attention back to him and Abby.

"Feel free to mingle around, and get anything you want to eat," Abby said. "The pool's out back; jump in whenever you're ready."

"Let's eat," Deke said, with a scowl on his face. I thought he was going to stomp a hole into the ground, the way he stormed to the picnic table.

"What's wrong?"

"Nothing," he said as he struggled with a plate. The way he looked, it was as if he had sucked a crate full of lemons.

"Are you sure? You look a little—"

"I don't like him, okay?" Deke spat out. "There's something about him I don't trust."

"You can't be serious," I said. "He's the nicest person out here. And he's black. That's more than I can say for little Miss Hostess. Have you noticed the way she looks at you? And how she drapes her arms around you every chance she gets?"

Deke plopped a spoonful of potato salad on his plate. "You read too much into little things. Everyone here is touchy-feely. That's just their nature."

"I wish Marcus would get touchy-feely with me."

Deke just sucked his teeth.

"Do you want to go swimming yet?" Deke asked again.

"Has it been thirty minutes already?" I asked. "I think we need fifteen more minutes."

"It's been an hour and a half."

I didn't bother arguing with him because I knew he was right. But every time Deke mentioned getting in the pool, my eyes focused in on all the full-chested, shapely girls frolicking about. If they were t-bone steaks, I was lucky to be a spare rib.

"Maxine, it is scorching out here."

I shrugged. "I'm fine."

"Deke, Maxine," someone called. I looked up. Abby was running to us.

"Y'all aren't going to get in the water?" she asked as she sat beside Deke. I watched and waited. Sure enough, she placed her hand on his arm.

"We were just talking about that," he said. He looked at me. "Are you getting in?"

"I don't think so," I said, my eyes planted on Abby's perfect chest. "I'm too tired to swim."

"What about you, Deke?" Abby asked. "Don't you want to get in the pool?"

"I don't know…"

"Come on," she said as she pulled him from his seat. "There's nothing wrong with getting a little wet."

Deke's eyes flashed open as she dragged him across the lawn to the pool. All the way there, he was trying to talk Abby into letting him go. I crossed my arms and stared at him. *He could try harder.*

"What are you staring at?"

I spun around. Marcus stood behind the table, looking like a Black Hercules. "Is he your boyfriend?" he asked, pointing to Deke.

"Who, Deke?" I laughed. "We're just good friends."

"That's nice to hear," he said. It was like he was burning a hole into me with his gaze.

I tried to shake off my nervousness. *Don't stare at him with a blank look; ask him something.* "What position do you play?" I stammered.

"Power Forward. You watch basketball?"

"Religiously," I said. I bit my lip. I watched basketball as much as I attended church.

"What's your favorite team?"

"Um, Clemson," I said. I was going to school there in the fall; it may as well be my favorite team.

"Yeah, they have a pretty good squad. But not as good as the Sooners will be once I start playing."

I tried not to look confused. *Who were the Sooners? And what were they trying to do so soon?*

"So, what is there to do in this town?" I asked.

"Not a hell of a lot."

Another plus—he curses.

He sat beside me. "But there is a town picnic tomorrow. Me and a few guys are going to it. You could come along with us if you want to."

What did you say—I could be your love slave?

"I'd love to," I said, before shaking my head. "But I've already made plans to go with someone else."

He arched an eyebrow. "You're dating already?"

"No, nothing like that. I'm going with Ja—with my father."

"I understand, you're trying to spend quality time with the old man. I wish me and my pop were as close."

At least you knew yours was alive.

"Marcus, can I ask you a question?" I didn't wait for him to respond. "How many black folks live in town?"

"Not a lot. There are only about forty or fifty at school. Of course, there are over fifteen hundred white kids there. But, with you and Deke, our numbers go up by two. Or should I say by one and a half."

I forced myself to laugh.

"I bet it's great to be mixed," he continued. "You can fit in any-where." He took a strand of my hair in his fingers. "If I didn't know any better, I'd think you were all black."

I looked down at my lap. "You'd be surprised how many people think the same thing," I said.

"Think what?" a voice said.

I looked up. Deke stood in front of us, dripping wet. Abby was at his side, holding his shirt.

"Oh, nothing," I said.

"I see," Deke replied. "You ready to go?"

I looked at my watch. "It isn't that late, is it?"

"It's late enough."

I sighed and stood. "Marcus, it was nice—"

"Are you sure you have to go so soon?" he asked. "If your friend, Derrick—"

"Deke," he said.

Marcus looked at him. "Sorry. I mean, if Deke wants to leave now, I can always drop you off later. It's no problem."

Deke stepped up and placed his hand on my arm. "Thanks, but no thanks." He began pulling me toward the car.

I waved at Marcus. "Maybe I'll see you tomorrow."

"I hope so," he replied.

"Bye, Deke," Abby yelled as Deke marched off. He quickly looked back at her and waved before continuing on.

He opened the door and leaped in the car. I was barely in myself before he started it up and pulled off.

"You could have at least dried off," I said.

"Not enough time."

I looked at my watch again. "It's not even eight-thirty," I said. "We told Jack we'd be back at ten."

"We may run into traffic."

"Traffic? Please," I said. "I'm surprised Abby didn't try to shackle you to her."

"The same could be said about Marcus."

"You sound jealous."

"You sound horny."

"Whatever," I said as I rolled my eyes. "Does Abby know about Yvonne?"

"What's there to know about her?"

"That she's your girlfriend."

Deke fell silent for a few seconds. "Yvonne and I broke up."

"Broke up? When?"

"Last night."

"But y'all have been together for over a year."

He nodded.

"Why didn't you say anything about it?"

"Because I didn't want to talk about it," he said. "You never liked her anyway."

"Can you blame me? She was so…good. Every time I heard her voice, I wanted to kick a dog or knock over a mailbox or something."

"What's wrong with being good?"

"Nothing, I guess. It just ain't me."

Deke smirked. "You're right about that."

"Very funny," I said as I pinched Deke's arm. "So Yvonne is out, and Abby is in."

"Isn't that the way it always goes?" he said, in a quieter tone.

Deke's eyes were soft and fragile, totally different from the harsh glare he shot me at Abby's house. His gaze seemed to peer through all the sarcasm, all of the sass that sheltered me.

I turned away from him and tried to extinguish the tiny flames popping up inside of me. "Y'all will get back together tomorrow. That's how it always is with you two."

"Not this time."

I stared at Deke. "You're serious, aren't you?"

"Yep."

"Why did you break up?"

Deke stole a glance at me, before turning back to the road. "We—I—have some issues I have to deal with."

"Like what?"

He shook his head. "Like I said, I don't want to talk about it."

Wait a minute, that was my line.

I sighed. "I guess there's nothing wrong with both of us making new friends."

Deke scoffed. "In high school, you weren't even thinking about dating. Now, one look at Marcus, and you're ready to marry the guy."

"High school was different. I wasn't interested in any immature, sex-on-the-brain, pimple-faced boys. Of course, by high school I was branded a lesbian, anorexic, femi-bitch. But that's not the point. Marcus is different. He's a lot more mature than those geeks back at home."

"He's a year younger than you," Deke said. "Not exactly what I'd call mature."

"Age isn't everything."

"Of course it isn't. I'm sure his physique has something to do with it."

"He's smart and fine," I said. "What more could a girl ask for? Anyway, why do you care? It's not like you're my bodyguard."

"Your mother did say—"

"I don't care what she said. I'm my own person, I can do whatever I want."

"If that's how you want it, fine!" he yelled.

"Fine!"

We rode for a few minutes in silence. Finally, I cleared my throat. "What's a Sooner?"

"Did y'all have fun?" Jack asked as we entered the house. He was stretched across the couch, reading a book. He pulled his glasses off and dropped them on the coffee table. "And where's your shirt?"

Deke looked down at his chest. He was so determined to leave Abby's house, I don't think he ever realized he wasn't wearing it. "It's a long story," he finally said. Little droplets of water fell to the floor as he walked through the room. "I'm going to sleep. Good night."

"Well, I had a good time," I said as I plopped down on the couch beside Jack. "It wasn't the best party I've been to, but we had the chance to meet a few people."

"Like who?" Jack asked.

I scratched my chin and pretended I couldn't remember his name. "I think his name was Marcus."

Jack sat up. "Marcus Thomas?"

Note to self: *Next time you meet a guy, find out his last name.*

"Really tall, dark-skinned? Plays basketball?" Jack asked.

I nodded. "That sounds like him. Do you know him?"

"Yeah, his dad and I are pretty good friends," he said. "Marcus is a fine young man. Smart and talented. Maybe he could show you around town."

He could show me around a pig sty for all I cared, as long as it was him doing the tour.

I looked around the living room. Everything there was ancient. Throwbacks from the Seventies, a turntable and a crate full of records, sat in one corner. It was the only thing not covered with a layer of dust.

I looked along the wall, hoping to see pictures of Jack, his family, or some part of his life. The only picture in the room was a baby picture of me.

"Jack, what do you have against Deke?"

"I think he's the one that has something against me."

I laughed. "Maybe both of you have chips on your shoulders."

Jack sat up in his chair and jutted his chin out. "I'm your father. I have the right to have a chip on my shoulder."

"According to Deke, fathers don't abandon their families."

Jack stared at me and slowly sighed. "I just don't trust the boy."

I rolled my eyes. There was a lot of mistrust going around lately, with Jack not trusting Deke and Deke not trusting Marcus. Deke and Jack must have both graduated with degrees in stupidity.

"Why not?" I asked. "It's not like we're having sex or anything. He's my best friend. I couldn't sleep with him even if I wanted to. And believe me, I don't want to."

At least, I didn't think I wanted to.

"I don't know…."

"What do you mean, 'you don't know?'" I asked. "Why can't you trust him? Or me, for that matter?"

"Maxine, you have to understand, I know how boys act. I used to be one once upon a time. Don't you see the way he treats you? It's not natural for a boy to be hovering around you like that and y'all not be physically involved. Is he gay?"

He did just break up with his girlfriend….

"No, he's not gay."

"Then what's his problem?"

"He doesn't sound like the one with the problem," I said, standing. "If you don't want to believe me, that's your business. I'm not arguing with you anymore about it." I turned and walked out of the room.

"Maxine," Jack called out.

I stuck my head back in the doorway.

"I'm sorry. I do believe you," he said. "I'm just being a typical father, I guess."

"Thanks," I said. "I know you only mean well."

"There is something else I wanted to talk about—that is, if you're not too tired."

I returned to the living room. The way Jack's voice sounded worried me.

"There's no easy way for me to tell you, so I may as well blurt it out." He took my hand. "I'm seeing someone right now. A woman. Her name is Veronica."

I kept a fake smile plastered to my face. I felt like he was betraying Mom.

"How serious is it?"

"We're engaged."

"Oh."

There were a few seconds of silence between us.

"Is that all you have to say?" he asked, still clutching my hand.

"What about Mom?"

"Kathy?" Jack frowned. "Your mother and I will never be together again."

The way he said it, so matter-of-factly, it felt as if he had no feelings for her.

"Don't you love her?" I asked.

"Of course I do," he said. "But not like before. There's too much bad blood between us. Your mother could never forgive me for…." His voice was quiet and low. "It just wouldn't work out."

I chewed on the bottom of my lip and tried to understand what Jack was saying now, and what Mom had said earlier that day. It was like having ice cream and hot fudge, and not being able to mix the two. It just wasn't fair.

Jack patted my hand. "I know you may be a little upset—"

"How does she look?"

"She's thin, with long black hair, and—"

"Is she white or black?"

His gaze dropped to his lap. "She's white."

I laughed. "Don't say it like you're ashamed. It's about time you stayed in your own race."

Jack's head jerked back up. "Do you only see things in terms of black and white? There is a lot more to most people than skin color. It was Dr. Martin Luther King that said—"

"Just like a white person. Every time y'all talk to a black person about race, y'all feel the need to bring up Dr. King."

"Dr. King was a great man."

"I'm not disputing that. All I'm saying is that y'all use Dr. King to feel less guilty about yourselves. All y'all white folks are the same."

"Maxine, you're white, too."

I opened my mouth, then shut it again. I couldn't think of anything to say.

"Kathy can't forgive me for killing a man and you can't forgive me for being white." Jack chuckled. "Is it too much to ask for both of you to hate me for the same thing?" He put his glasses back on and picked up his book. "Anyway, I wanted to warn you about Veronica before the picnic tomorrow. She and Sheila will be there."

I crossed my arms. "And who is Sheila?"

"Her daughter."

"Is she yours?"

"You're my only child," he said.

"Thank God for small miracles," I said as I rolled my eyes and left the room.

I needed to push thoughts of my soon-to-be stepmother out of my mind, so I stopped in front of Deke's room and knocked on the door.

"Come in."

I stuck my head inside the room, and tried to avert my eyes from his shirtless chest. "One quick question. Would you rather watch the World Series or go to the ballet?"

Before I could close the door, a pillow flew across the room and smashed into my face.

"At least some things aren't a surprise," I said.

CHAPTER 10

I felt like an entire loaf of bread that had been stuffed into a toaster, as I sat sandwiched between Deke and Jack in the truck. We left a trail of dust and dirt in our wake as we made our way down an old country road to the town picnic.

Finally we pulled into a clearing. The gravel lot was full of assorted cars and trucks. Beyond the lot sat rows of picnic tables, each piled with food. Chicken, corn on the cob, hamburgers, ribs—I smelled everything as I stepped out of the truck. I caught myself drooling, the food smelled so good.

I watched as other families walked from their cars to the picnic tables, each with armloads of food. "Jack, we didn't bring anything to eat."

"I know," he said as we walked to the tables. "We didn't have to bring anything."

"Let me guess, the ladies from the church brought enough food for everyone." I folded my arms. "Or better yet, Veronica, the good little housewife, cooked enough food."

"You'll see," Jack said. "We're almost there."

We walked a few more yards before stopping at one of the rear tables. Like the others, it was filled with food—bowls of barbecue, potato salad, baked beans, cole slaw—all you could eat. I looked around, expecting to see Veronica.

"Hi, Jack," a black woman a few feet away said. She was short and plump, with curly black hair and a gentle face.

I frowned at her. Either Jack's fiancée had a great tan and had gained some weight, or this wasn't Veronica.

"Hi, Georgia," Jack said as he embraced the woman. "Where's that excuse for a husband of yours?"

"Right behind you," he said. We turned around. A tall, well-built man stood behind us. My mouth dropped open once I saw Marcus Thomas standing beside him.

"Long time no see," Marcus said.

I stared at Marcus. *Why didn't they make boys like that in South Carolina?*

All last night, I dreamed of him. And me. *Together.* I was almost ashamed of where I found my hand when I woke up.

Jack wrapped his arm around me. "Maxine, I'd like you to meet my good friends, Bobby Joe Thomas and his wife, Georgia. You've already met Marcus."

Bobby Joe took my hand. "Marcus wasn't lying when he said you were beautiful."

I shook Bobby Joe's hand, but looked at Marcus. He just winked at me.

Can I have your baby?

Georgia stood in front of me. I raised my hand, expecting her to shake it. Instead, she reached out and hugged me.

"Jack's family is our family," she said as she released me and looked at me. "Girl, what are they feeding you in South Carolina? You got to get some meat on your bones."

As Deke and Marcus's family exchanged greetings, two children ran up to the table. The boy looked to be about ten and the girl couldn't be older than six. They were both covered in dust. Georgia grabbed both of them with one hand and proceeded to brush them off with the other.

Marcus and I pulled away from the group. "Is that your brother and sister?" I asked.

"Unfortunately," he said. "I try to disown them as much as possible."

"They don't look that bad."

"You try living with them for half of your life. Do you have any brothers or sisters?"

"Nope, just me."

"You're so lucky," he said, eyeing the children once more. Then he looked at Deke. "I see you brought your friend out here."

"Of course. He's my best friend. I had to drag someone out here with me."

"So, are y'all fucking?"

Did everyone around here share a brain or something? First Jack thought we were sleeping together and now Marcus thought the same thing. I shook my head. "Like I said before, we're only friends."

"Good," he said. "Now I won't feel bad stealing you away from him."

I laughed. "Oh, so you're some type of womanizer."

Marcus flashed me his billion-dollar smile. "What? Me, a womanizer?" He wrapped his arm around me. "Anyway, Deke will probably be too busy messing with Abby to worry about us." He leaned closer to me. "You know, she gives it up on the first night."

I tried to ignore the goose bumps forming on my arms. "Sleeping with someone after knowing them for a day isn't exactly ladylike."

"Are you ladylike?"

"Wouldn't you like to know," I said as I flung his arm off me. "Let's eat, I'm starving."

I looked back toward the table, and wouldn't you know it, Abby was talking to Deke. I marched over and crammed myself between them.

"Oh, Maxine," Abby said. "We were just talking about you."

"Umph. I'll bet."

"I wonder if the food is almost ready," Deke said, smiling weakly at me. "I haven't eaten all day."

"Are y'all eating over here?" Abby asked, pointing to the table. Deke and I nodded.

"Is there enough room for all of you at the table?" she asked. "If not, you could always eat with us, Deke."

I crossed my arms. "Thanks for the hospitality, but we have plenty of room."

"Are you sure?" she asked. "It's not a big deal."

"What's not a big deal?" Marcus said as he, Jack and Bobby Joe walked up. "Abby, you want to eat with us?"

She shook her head. "No, my family is over there. I was inviting Deke to sit with us."

"And I was just telling her that we had enough room for everyone," I snapped. I didn't care if I had to eat on the ground with the ants. Deke was not going to spend time with Abby. Not if I had anything to do about it.

"We *are* running a little low on space, especially with Veronica and Sheila coming," Jack said. "Deke, would you mind sitting with Abby?"

"He doesn't mind," Marcus said. His eyes narrowed as he stared at him. "Do you?"

Deke looked at me before shaking his head. "I don't mind."

"Great, it's settled then," Abby hooked Deke with her arm. "We'll be right over there."

I grabbed Deke's other arm and pulled him away from her. "Hold on a second. Deke, can I speak to you?"

Deke and I walked away from the group. He rubbed at his shoulder.

"Next time, you don't have to pull my arm out of its socket."

I planted myself in front of him. "I know you aren't going to eat dinner with her."

"Apparently, some people don't want me at the table."

I looked back at Jack and Marcus. They looked like long lost friends, catching up on old times.

"Don't blame this on them," I said. "Abby was the one that started this mess in the first place."

"It doesn't matter. I'm sure you can get along a few minutes without me."

"It's not *me* I'm worried about."

"Is that why you're making such a big deal about this?" he asked. "You don't see me making a scene about you and Marcus."

"That's different."

"How?"

"For one, he isn't a sex crazed slut like she is," I said, pointing to Abby.

Deke yanked me further away from the group. "Maybe you should talk a little louder, Maxine. I don't think they heard you in Canada."

I poked Deke in the chest. "You just make sure you don't get caught in her little trap."

"And you just try to behave yourself."

I nodded, and we walked back to the group. Abby immediately wrapped her arm around him again. Deke just looked back at me while she dragged him off.

"Where is Veronica," I said. "It's kinda rude for her to be so late, isn't it?"

Jack shook his head and pointed. "There she is."

I watched as a tall, perfectly shaped, pale-looking woman walked toward the table. Her black hair sat elegantly on her head, accentuating her beauty even more. Compared to her hair, mine looked like the fur of a mangy dog.

Her smile grew as she got closer to us. I looked at Jack. His eyes were glazed over. Sickening.

"You must be Maxine," she said as she stood before me. "I'm Veronica."

I reluctantly shook her hand. Her skin was covered with little freckles. It was like she had never gotten over the chicken pox.

"Where is Sheila," Jack asked. "I thought she was coming."

Veronica leaned closer to Jack. "No, she had a…doctor's appointment today," she whispered.

Maybe having a sister wasn't that bad, I thought. By her not showing up, hopefully there was room for Deke after all. I hadn't even met her yet, and already my step-sister was coming to my rescue.

I moved toward them. "I should get Deke," I said. "I'm sure we have enough room for him now."

Jack shook his head. "He'll be fine."

"But—"

"We still don't have enough room at the table," Jack said. "You can survive without Deke for one meal." He headed toward the table. "Come on, the food is getting cold."

Before I could come up with a good rebuttal, everyone was seated at the table. As much as I hated to admit it, there really wasn't enough room for all of us. I squeezed in between Jack and Marcus, and across from Veronica. Marcus grinned as my thigh rubbed against his. I looked down at his and my legs. My legs looked like chalk compared to his dark skin.

"Let's bless the food," Bobby Joe said. On cue, everyone bowed their heads. "Would anyone like to say grace?"

Marcus nodded and began praying. During the entire blessing, I kept spying on Deke and Abby. She was practically throwing herself at him. I thought she would poke his eye out with one of her breasts.

Marcus finished the blessing and we began fixing our food. I took as little of each thing as possible. I needed to finish quickly so I could go rescue Deke.

"Jack tells us you're going to Clemson in the fall," Bobby Joe said.

I didn't have time for conversation. I just nodded as I shoveled a heap of cole slaw into my mouth.

"A recruiter from Clemson came out here this year to look at Marcus play." Bobby Joe beamed at his son. "You know, every college wants him. He's that good."

Marcus sat up. "No, I'm better."

The conversation continued to center around Marcus and how great he was. Don't get me wrong, I liked Marcus as much as the next guy. But, the way they talked, you'd think he was the best thing to happen since the Emancipation Proclamation. I would have given anything for someone to change the subject.

"So, when is the wedding?" Georgia asked.

Great. And I thought the topic of conversation couldn't get worse....

"Next spring," Veronica flashed a smile at Jack. "I hope."

"Are you going to be in the wedding?"

It was a couple of seconds before I realized Bobby Joe was talking to me. I bit my lip and looked at Jack. "Well…"

"Of course she is," Jack said. "Both of our daughters are going to be in the wedding."

"Like hell," I mumbled.

Apparently, my statement wasn't quite a mumble. Everyone at the table froze, forks in mid-air, staring at me. I felt like an animal on display at the zoo.

"I mean, hell yeah, I'm going to be in the wedding!"

Jack groaned. "Maxine, you're not making it any better. Just finish your food."

We finished our food in clumsy silence, interspersed with awkward small talk. Not that I cared about having upset anyone. I had other things to worry about, like saving Deke from that hussy.

"Georgia, Bobby Joe, thank you for the dinner," Veronica said as she rose. "I wish I could stay longer, but I really have to get going. Sheila is waiting for me."

Jack stood from the table as well. "Are we still on for tomorrow afternoon?" he asked as he neared her.

"If you think that's best."

He stole a quick glance at me. "Everything will be fine. We'll see you tomorrow after church."

Veronica looked at me. "I look forward to getting to know you a lot better, Maxine."

"Um, yeah," I said, quickly shaking her hand. I watched as Jack escorted her to the car. He reminded me of a chicken, the way he pecked her cheek, just before she stepped into the car. I laughed to myself. *Wait until I tell Deke*—

I stared at the table where he had been sitting. It was empty. I looked around the entire picnic area, but I didn't see him.

"What's wrong with you?" Marcus asked.

"I can't find Deke." I began walking off. "When Jack gets back, tell him I went for a walk."

"Hey, wait up," he said, running behind me. "Let me walk with you."

"But—"

"Don't try to argue with me," he said. "You'll find that I don't like taking no for an answer."

I just sighed and we began down a trail. "Are trees the only thing around here, or are there any mutant cows walking around?"

"You're pretty sarcastic," he said.

"It's the only way to be."

He slid his hand onto the small of my back. "Well, I like my women with a little sass."

"And what makes you think I'm your woman?"

Marcus's tongue darted across his lips. "You're right, you aren't my woman. But the summer is still young."

"You're bold, I'll give you that much," I said.

"Not bold," he said. "I just know what I want." He led me down another path. "There's a natural spring not too far from here. I can show it to you."

"We're supposed to be looking for Deke."

"He's probably out here with Abby."

A small shudder ran through me as I pictured them together. "You don't know Deke," I said. "He won't waste his time with a girl like her."

"I don't know," he said. "They looked pretty friendly when they left the table."

"Looks can be deceiving," I said. I reached into my pocket and pulled out a wad of money. "I'll bet you thirty bucks he won't even touch her."

He frowned. "Are you that anxious to lose your money?"

"Are you too scared to take a bet?"

Marcus shrugged. "Okay, just don't be mad when you lose."

We slowed our steps. The path had become narrow, and was overgrown with lush vegetation. At one stretch, the path was so thin, we had to travel in single file. I could almost feel Marcus's gaze on my butt as I walked ahead of him.

"Was this your first time meeting Veronica?" I asked.

"No, I see her all the time. She's a Deaconess at the church."

I should have known...

"Sheila, her daughter, is a year younger than me," he continued. "A real brainy kid. But real weird."

"What do you mean, weird?"

"Shhh," Marcus said. He crept off of the trail and behind some large rocks. In the background, I heard the flow of water. A little less obvious was the sound of laughter.

I knelt beside Marcus and peered over a boulder. Deke and Abby sat beside each other in the grass by the spring. Actually, it was more like they sat on top of each other.

I could read Marcus's mind. "Just because they're sitting close together doesn't mean anything," I said.

"That's damn close. And what is her hand doing on his crotch?"

I slapped his arm. "That's not funny."

He was still looking at Deke and Abby. "Well, what do you think about that?"

I turned back around. Deke and Abby were kissing. Hard.

Before I halfway realized it myself, I had climbed over the boulder and was making a beeline for Abby and Deke. Apparently, they were so into each other, they didn't notice me until I was right in front of them. Deke looked up just in time to see me snatch him away from her.

"What the—" Abby began. "What's your goddamn problem?"

I planted my fists on my hips. "Damn, girl," I said, staring her down. "What will you *not* do to get a man?"

"Listen, bitch—"

"Oh, that's it! I'm about to whip your ass!"

Just as I was about to connect with Abby's face, Deke caught me and pulled me away. "Both of you, calm down."

I struggled to pull away from him, but there was no way my little frame was getting out of his grasp.

"Maxine, stop it," Deke said. "This isn't like you."

"Look who's talking."

By now, Marcus had made his way over to us. "Is everything all right?"

"That bitch was about to get her damn head knocked off," Abby said.

I lunged at her. "Call me a bitch again, and we'll see whose head gets knocked off!"

Deke kept a tight grip on me. "Abby, I apologize for this. She usually isn't this way." He looked at Marcus. "I'm going to walk Abby back. We'll see y'all at the picnic area."

Deke slowly let go of me, and he and Abby walked down the trail. Trying not to pout, I collapsed on the ground and tugged at a blade of grass.

"Are you okay?" Marcus asked.

"I'll survive." I fished into my pocket and pulled out the money. "I guess this is yours."

He sat down beside me and took it. He flipped through it, before sticking it back into my pocket. "I'll trade you for it."

"For what?" I asked.

By now his face was inches from mine. He brushed a strand of hair out of my face and looked at my mouth. He quickly licked his lips before pressing them against mine.

Hmmm, sugary.

Seconds later, he slipped his tongue in my mouth. Well, more like shoved. I almost gagged at first.

We continued kissing, maybe for minutes. Then suddenly, I pulled away.

"What?" he asked. "Is there a problem?"

"Um, yeah. It's getting late." I looked down at my chest. "And your hand is on my breast."

He removed his hand and placed in on my thigh. It slowly crept up my leg. "I could always put it somewhere else."

"Not if you ever want to have children."

His hand froze. "Maybe we should go back."

We returned to the picnic area, where the celebration was in full swing. I searched through the crowd and finally saw Deke, sitting alone at a table.

I ran up to him. "Where's the tramp?"

He looked at me for a long time, as if he was memorizing the very texture of my face. His eyes were like a void. I stared into them, but I couldn't figure out what he was thinking.

I crossed my arms. "Aren't you going to say anything?"

He slowly rose from his seat like a balloon that had lost most of its helium. He chewed on his lip for a second before doing something he had never done before: he turned and just walked away.

CHAPTER 11

"Is that what you're wearing?" Jack asked.

I stopped in the hallway and looked down at myself. My sneakers were caked with dirt and mud. My jeans were frayed at the ends, and slivers of caramel-coated skin were beginning to show through at my knees. My t-shirt was something I was particularly proud of. I had picked it up at the flea market a couple of years ago and saved it for a special occasion, such as this. It said *Satan Rules*.

I shrugged. "What's wrong with this?"

"You're going to church, not to a rock concert."

The idea of going to a rock concert made me laugh. "What's wrong with what I have on?" I said, giving him a sly smile. "Unfortunately, I didn't pack any dresses. Maybe I shouldn't even go to church."

He crossed his arms. "Go and change into something else."

"But—"

"Go. Now."

I hung my head a little, trudged back to my room, and kicked off my shoes, causing them to fly to the ceiling. Going to church was about as appealing as getting a root canal. I hated the idea of a preacher standing in the pulpit, looking so high and mighty in his flashy robe, spewing down hell and brimstone. What right did he have to tell me what God wanted us to do? I was pretty sure he'd never been up to heaven for coffee and cake.

I tugged at my jeans and threw them across the room, so that they landed on top of my sneakers. I yanked my khakis out of the closet and slipped them on. I stopped pulling them up to look at the spot where Marcus had palmed my thigh. I felt myself getting warm as I thought about him. Maybe it wouldn't be that bad if he and I —

"Hurry up. We're going to be late," Jack said.

I buckled my pants and grabbed a blouse. "I don't want you to be late, so if you have to, leave without me."

"Maxine," Jack said, sighing. "Just hurry up."

I threw my blouse on and walked out of the door. Jack stood positioned at the door, with his hand resting on the handle. He smiled when I walked into the kitchen. "You look very pretty, like your mother."

I couldn't help smiling. Mom was beautiful. She could fill out a pair of jeans like nobody's business. Every time we went out together, I saw how every man in the area seemed to drool over her. Their eyes floated all over her body. Mom shrugged it off, saying that men will be men. I think she thought it was demeaning the way men ogled at her. If anything, I was jealous.

"Where's Deke?" I said, looking behind me. I knew that he wasn't about to miss the next episode of "God and the Holy Rollers."

"He went to Sunday School."

Figures.

I followed Jack out of the door and climbed into the truck. As he climbed in beside me, I took the time to check him out. He wore a simple blue suit and a matching tie.

He hummed quietly as he pulled out of the driveway. I strained to hear the tune he was mumbling, but couldn't quite catch it.

"What are you humming?" I finally asked.

"Amazing Graze," he said, taking a quick break from his humming.

I let him hum a few more bars before I joined in. He looked at me with a surprised expression.

"You know the words to Amazing Grace?"

"Just because I don't go to church doesn't mean I've never heard a hymn or two before," I said. "Mom sings it all the time."

"Kathy always did love that song." He frowned. "If you knew the song, why did you ask me what I was humming?"

"Well, to be honest, you don't exactly have the best singing voice. And it helps that Mom usually enunciates."

He laughed. "Your mother had such a great voice. When she used to sing, she would get this look on her face, like there were a million smiles hiding in her lips. She made you hang on to each word, each syllable that she sang. It sounded so sweet; almost angelic. And she made it look so easy."

I nodded at Jack's words. I had seen that look on Mom's face from time to time as she sang softly to herself while bumbling around in the kitchen. Sometimes, if I was really quiet, I could sneak into the kitchen while she sang. And did she sing. Her back would arch slightly, and she would close her eyes and look up, with the same expression that Jack just described.

"I met your mother through music. We used to be in a little jazz band together."

My mouth dropped to the floor. "Mom never told me that."

"She was the lead singer," he continued. "You should hear her sing some of those old tunes. It was like a fine wine to the ears. Smooth and savory. It could melt your soul if you weren't careful."

I pictured Mom in a smoky café, with a black strapless dress on, crooning to the crowd in front of her. I could almost hear her voice—sweet with just a touch of raspiness.

"What did you do? I know you didn't sing."

He laughed, but it was a hollow laugh. His gaze fell to his fingers on the steering wheel. They were old fingers; knotty, veined, and scarred from age and whatever life had thrown at him.

"I was the piano player."

When I was a child, I had wanted to take piano lessons. At the time, all the other pretty, popular girls were taking them, so I wanted to as well. I asked Mom and she refused outright. I actually thought she hated me by the way she acted. She ended up enrolling me in a karate class, where I learned the sacred art of kicking boys in the groin.

Jack pulled into the church parking lot. It was packed full of people. Half of the women wore hats big enough for helicopters to land on. I swear, some of them had to turn their heads to the side just to get through the doorway.

Jack led me inside the sanctuary and pointed to Deke. I started down the aisle, but stopped when I noticed that Jack wasn't following me. "Where are you going?" I asked.

He nodded toward the front of the church. "Up there, with the other deacons."

"Oh," I said as I watched him walk away. I tried to shrug the feeling of queasiness off. Why was I being so paranoid? It's not like he's going to be sitting on the other side of world, right?

I slipped into the pew and sat beside Deke. I peeked at him out of the corner of my eye. We hadn't spoken to each other since the other night.

I began to speak, but instead looked down at my lap. I could feel him staring at me. Was he mad? I didn't mean to embarrass him. I just felt—*how did I feel?*

"Listen, Deke," I began.

"Shhh," he whispered, before smiling. "After church."

I smiled back at him, and was almost inclined to grab his hand. *Almost.* I did have a reputation to protect.

Jack sat with a group of men to the side of the pulpit. Most were dressed like he was, in simple suits. Some of the older ones looked like rejects from the eighteenth century. How could they hear with all of that hair growing out of their ears?

I continued to look around the church. My gaze stopped on the choir stand. Abby sat on the first row, with her best innocent look on her face.

I could almost picture myself knocking her teeth out.

A few seats up from her sat Marcus. He winked at me. I felt myself beaming and stopped myself. The last thing I wanted to do was to let that boy think he had me wrapped around his finger. Or wrapped around something worse.

There were only a few black people in the church. Bobby Joe and his family sat a few rows ahead of us. I turned around and counted three more couples. I looked at Deke. Four more, including us.

"Can we sit here?"

I turned around to see Veronica standing beside me. A teenage girl, whom I assumed to be Sheila, stood behind her. I had been so busy scoping out the church, I didn't even see them walk up.

Veronica flashed a toothy smile as she clutched her Bible in her pale, spotted hands. The expression on Sheila's face shouted that she'd rather be any place but here. Deke and I slid over.

Veronica wore a yellow dress that stopped mid-calf. Her hat wasn't as big or as loud as some of the other ladies' hats, but it was there nevertheless. Sheila was a much shorter, much plumper version of her mother. Her stout legs seemed to poke out awkwardly from under her black and white dress. She reminded me of an overgrown penguin as she waddled into the pew.

"I'm glad you could make it out today," Veronica said, after she sat down. "I didn't know if you would be in attendance."

"And what gave you that idea?"

Veronica's mouth dropped open. "Um, well...you know."

"No, I don't."

Veronica leaned closer to my ear. "With your religious beliefs and all."

"I don't mind coming to church," I said as my voice got louder, "even though I don't waste my time praying to God."

There were some slight murmurs around me, and a large groan from beside me. I didn't even have to look to know Deke had a scowl on his face.

"Umm, I think the service is about to begin," Veronica stammered.

A woman came to the front of the church. She started rambling off announcements and I quickly lost interest. Then, she asked for all the visitors to stand.

Deke began to stand up, but I pulled him back down. "What are you doing?" I whispered to him.

"I'm standing up. We're visitors, remember."

"I'm not getting up."

He shrugged. "Suit yourself." He stood along with the other visitors in the church.

I sat back in the pew and crossed my arms. *Well, he can do whatever he wants to do, but I'm still not standing up.* I looked at the front of the church, and Jack's gaze met mine. I tried to pretend that I didn't notice him, but I could feel his eyes on me. Reluctantly, I stood up.

Deke whispered in my ear, "Do you want me to speak for both of us?"

I rolled my eyes. "I did graduate from high school. I think I can speak for myself."

He nodded and turned to the front of the church. Slowly each visitor said a little bit about himself or herself, and sat down. As I listened to them, I realized I didn't know what to say. Just as I opened my mouth to say something to Deke, the woman at the front of the church nodded at him.

"Hello, my name is Deke Ashland, and I'm from Columbia, South Carolina. I bring greetings from Pastor Eugene Hammond and Mount Zion Baptist Church. I'm here visiting with Deacon Phillips, and I just want to thank y'all for making me feel welcome."

A few of the members groaned "Amen" as Deke sat down. I stared at the woman as she nodded at me. I turned around to make sure she wasn't nodding at someone else. I was the only person standing.

I cleared my throat. "Hi, my name is Maxine Phillips. I am also from South Carolina, and I am here visiting my father, Deacon Phillips. Um...I am a member of...Greater Saint Mary Southern Baptist Cathedral, where the pastor is...Reverend Jesse Jackson King...Jr."

I sat back down, but immediately bounced back up. "And I'm also glad to be here."

That wasn't bad, I thought to myself as I eased into my seat. I looked at Jack. Why did he look like he was having a stroke?

The woman at the front of the church took her seat, and a big, swaggering man came to the podium. I could see the glistening of his gold watch and matching cuff links from my seat. His hair looked like it had been drowned in mousse. His suit by itself looked more expensive than half of the deacons' suits put together. He gripped the edges of the podium with his big hands and peered at the congregation.

"Welcome to the house of the Lord. Now, please prepare yourselves for the tithe and offering."

CHAPTER 12

I bit my lip and waited for Deke to turn off the car. He hadn't said a word during the trip from church, but I knew he wanted to say something. Or, wanted to hear something.

"Listen," I began, "about yesterday, I know you must think I'm crazy—"

"Among other things."

I sighed. "And what were you doing kissing her, anyway? Didn't you just break up with your girlfriend?"

"I can't believe you're acting like I was the bad guy," Deke said.

"Well…"

"Well, nothing. You have no right interfering in my personal life like that."

"Why not?" I asked. "You always interfere in mine."

"Giving someone advice and trying to bash someone's head in are two different things."

I squirmed in my seat. "You never answered my question. What were you doing kissing her? What about those issues you're supposed to be dealing with?"

Deke shook his head. "Are you going to apologize or not?"

I rolled my eyes. "Okay, sorry."

Deke crossed his arms. "Say it like you mean it."

"But I—"

"Say it."

I looked at him. His eyes were unwavering. "Deke, I'm sorry if I embarrassed you and made you look like a fool. I will never do it again."

Deke scowled. "You really need to work on your apologies."

"I haven't had much practice. Now talk."

Deke smiled, and I knew everything was okay. "It was a kiss, simple as that. Abby isn't all that bad."

"She's white," I said.

"So what."

"You're selling out."

"Just because she's white doesn't mean I'm selling out. I'm just as black as I was last week."

That was more than I could say about myself.

"Why do you have to date someone white, Deke? Are you saying that there aren't any other black girls you find attractive?"

"No," Deke said, with a quiet voice. "I didn't say that."

"Then leave that white girl alone."

He frowned. "You're bordering on racist."

"Black people can't be racist; it's a proven fact," I said. "Prejudiced, yeah. Racist, no."

"Anyone can be racist."

I pushed myself up in my seat. "Well, my brotha, are you going to see her anymore?"

He didn't say anything for a minute. "Yeah. This evening."

"Okay, OJ," I said. "I've got a pair of gloves in the house, if you need them."

Deke's nostrils became flared. "I'm not going to sit here and listen to this," he said as he opened the car door. "You sound like you belong to the Nation of Islam."

"You sound like you belong in Beverly Hills."

Deke stepped out of the car and slammed the door shut so hard, my teeth shook. He seemed to punish the concrete with every angry stride he took away from the car.

Good going, Maxine. You just called your best friend an Uncle Tom. And I was the one that was mixed. *What was that about the pot calling the kettle black...?* I followed him out of the car.

"Now what?" he yelled as I neared him. "Am I too black to stare across the street?"

"Deke, I'm sorry," I began. "I didn't mean what I said back there. It's just that everything is really crazy right now. It's like the black part of me hates the white part of me and vice versa." I chuckled. "It's like I hate myself for being me."

"Don't hate yourself," he said. "You're too beautiful for that."

Out of nowhere, those little tingles popped up again. They were like sparks of electricity, exploding all along my body. "I'll be fine," I said, turning my gaze away from him. "Let's worry about you."

"There's nothing to worry about."

"Then why did you break up with Yvonne?" I asked.

Deke looked at his watch. "Shouldn't Jack be here by now? Maybe we should call him."

No way are you getting away that easy. "Was she cheating on you?"

"He must have gotten held up at the church."

"Were you cheating on her?"

There was a slight pause. "What's your definition of cheating?"

My eyes flashed open. "Deke, don't tell me you—"

"While I was with Yvonne, I never once kissed, touched, or did anything else with another girl."

I leaned closer. "So, you're saying that you didn't cheat on her?"

Deke bowed his head and sighed. "What I'm trying to say…."

Deke's voice trailed off as Jack's truck rumbled down the street. Jack parked and jumped out of the truck. "Didn't I give you a key?" he asked me.

"Um…I must have left it inside."

Jack eyed me and Deke. We were extremely close to each other by now; close enough to kiss if we so desired. Deke must have noticed too, because he immediately took a few steps away from me.

"Come on inside," Jack said as he walked between us, almost pushing Deke over. "Veronica will be over any minute for dinner."

After Jack disappeared into the house, Deke turned to me. "You heard the man. Let's go."

"Wait. We're not finished talking."

"Yes, we are." He walked toward the house.

I crossed my arms. "No, we aren't."

Deke opened the door. "You can stay out here and talk to yourself all day if you want, but I'm going in." He stepped inside the house and closed the door.

I stood by the steps for a few moments and waited for him to walk back outside. After ten minutes in the sweltering heat, I finally followed him in.

I hate it when I'm wrong.

I had just nestled myself into a soft spot on the bed, when there was a short rap at my door. I dropped my magazine. "Come in."

Jack cracked the door open. "Veronica and Sheila are here. Why don't you come out and keep them company?"

"I'd rather be smothered in butter and grilled over an open flame."

"That's nice, honey. See you in five minutes."

Jack closed the door before I had the chance to say anything else. I shrugged. What could it hurt? They were practically family.

I dragged myself to the kitchen, where Veronica, Sheila, and Jack were busy unwrapping containers of food. Veronica stopped once she noticed I had entered the room. "Hi, Maxine. Hope you like fried chicken."

I plastered a smile to my face. "Don't you know, all black people like fried chicken. We put it right up there with watermelon."

Sheila was the only one who laughed. Veronica fanned at herself and stared at Jack out of the corner of her eye.

"I'm going to the store," Jack said as he turned to Sheila. "Do you want to come along for the ride?"

"What is this, 'Get to know your stepchild day?'" Sheila asked as she rose from the table. "I may as well go with you. I'm sure if I said no, y'all would make me go anyway."

As soon as Jack and Sheila left, Veronica turned her attention to dinner. I was amazed at how natural she looked in the kitchen. It was as if her body had been possessed by one of those late night cooking gurus. As she sifted flour, not a drop was spilled. As she poured rice, every grain fell into the pot. She didn't need any measuring cups; she automatically seemed to know when enough was enough.

"What did you think about the service?" Veronica asked.

"Okay, I guess. I don't have much to compare it to," I said. "I didn't really like Pastor—what's his name?"

"Pastor Griggs. Jack doesn't particularly care for him either. Jack says Griggs seems more interested in raising money than preaching the word."

"If Jack doesn't like him, why doesn't he leave? I'm sure he could find another church."

Her gaze stayed on me as she cracked an egg open. "Jack won't move to another church. First United is like a family to him. He won't leave now, especially in these troubling times."

"Troubling times? What do you mean?"

Veronica wiped her hands on a dishtowel. "We've been losing a lot of members lately. Many of them don't agree with Pastor Griggs style of preaching and would rather attend another church. And to be honest, most of those members were of the wealthier persuasion. The church has had to resort to car washes and bake sales to bring in extra cash. If we don't start bringing back members—and quickly—there may be no more First United," she said. "And that would kill Jack."

"I still don't understand. Why is that church so special? And if things are so bad, why doesn't he get up and preach? Isn't that what he went to school for?"

"It's more complicated than that."

"What do you mean?"

Veronica shook her head. "You'll have to talk to your father about that."

Thanks a lot, Mom.

I sat at the table and stared at everyone. Not exactly what I would call a traditional family. Jack kept rubbing his hands together and watching Veronica. Sheila seemed as if she was lost in her own private universe. And Deke—I just couldn't bring myself to look at him. Not after our non-talk outside.

Jack blessed the meal and we began to pass the food around. I took the chicken and passed it to Sheila. She looked at it like it was the black plaque and passed it on to her mother.

"I wish you hadn't cooked chicken," Sheila said, wiping her fingers on her napkin. "That food was a living, breathing thing once."

Veronica dropped a chicken leg on her plate. "Sheila, please don't start."

"Why don't you eat meat?" I asked.

"I'm rebelling against apartheid in South Africa. I'm not eating meat until Nelson Mandela is freed and blacks are allowed to run the government."

"Um, I think you're a little late," I said.

She looked at me, then at Deke. "What about the end of communism in the Soviet Union?"

"Ended in Ninety-One," he replied.

She sighed. "Then I just don't like the taste of it."

I shook my head and shoveled some rice onto my plate. No question about it, her parents must have been related.

"What do you guys think of the town so far?" Veronica asked, after everyone had fixed their food. "I hope it isn't too small for you."

"It's nice," Deke said. "We met some of the kids from the church the other day, and most of them seem pretty nice. I'm supposed to meet one of the girls—Abby—today after dinner. We're going to the movies."

Jack smiled. "That's nice. Abby is a sweet girl."

"Umph," I said. "Sheila, do you know Abby?"

"We attend the same school," she said. She seemed to have a little twinkle in her eye.

I crossed my arms. "What do you think of her? Honestly."

"Most of the guys seem to like her." She stole a quick glance at her mother. "But personally, I think she's a bitch."

"Sheila!" Veronica exclaimed. "What has gotten into you?"

Sheila shrugged. "Must be the chicken."

"I don't want to hear one more word from you. Do you understand?" Veronica was standing, violently shaking her fork at her.

Sheila flashed me a quick smile, showing off a mouthful of braces. I smiled back. That girl had style.

Jack cleared his throat. "Let's just finish our dinner."

I took a bite of chicken. "Yeah, Jack, I guess you're beginning to rub off on Deke. He's got the fever, just like you did."

"Maxine, please," Deke whimpered.

"Are you sick?" Veronica asked, looking at Deke. She reached over and touched his head. "You don't feel hot."

"Not that type of fever, Mom. She's talking about Jungle Fever."

Veronica frowned. "Jungle Fever?"

Deke began to sink into his chair.

Sheila put her fork down in her plate and wiped her mouth. "Basically, he likes fucking white girls."

The entire table fell silent.

And I thought *I* was bold.

After dinner, I excused myself and walked out onto the porch. The light summer breeze stirred my wild locks. Sheila looked up as I neared the swing.

"Can I sit down?"

She nodded, so I plopped down beside her. "Not that I'm complaining, but you're pretty ballsy for a sixteen-year-old," I said. "Sorry you didn't get a chance to finish dinner."

"It's okay. I ate three candy bars on the way here, so I'm not hungry." She pushed against the floor and put the swing into motion. "I see you don't like Abby that much."

"What makes you say that?" I asked. "You're the one that made the wild comment."

"True. But the expression on your face when Deke said that he was going out with her was far worse than anything I could have said."

I nodded and cracked a smile. "She is a little slut, isn't she?"

"She's the best at what she does. Sleeping around."

I sighed. "What does Deke see in her? Why would he go out with someone like that?"

"That's obvious," she said. "Easy sex."

I shook my head. "Deke's not like that."

"Every guy is like that."

"Deke's not every guy."

Sheila frowned. "Why haven't you two hooked up?"

"We're just friends."

"Friends as in bed buddies?" she asked.

I rolled my eyes. "No, just friends."

"And who's idea was that? His?"

"No, it's just the way things are," I said. "What makes you think he's the one that wanted us to be only friends?"

"You seem kinda jealous, that's all."

I snorted. "Jealous? Please." I searched for some snappy comeback line, but couldn't think of one. "Anyway, I'm more interested in Marcus."

"Marcus? Not to burst your bubble, but he's as much of a slut as Abby is."

I pressed my lips together. "He is not. How would you know?"

"I've known the boy ever since I was born," she said. "Believe me when I tell you, he's a sexoholic. Of course, most kids at my age are…."

"And what about you?" I asked.

"I'm just a normal kid."

I laughed. "Normal is the last word I would use to describe you."

She laughed, too. "You aren't half bad. Not the girl I was expecting to meet."

I had to admit, I liked Sheila as well. It was hard not to like a girl that was so…colorful.

"So, what do you think about them?" I said, pointing back toward the house.

"You mean Mom and Jack."

I nodded.

"I don't have a big problem with them getting married," she said. "God knows, I've seen worse. Jack seems to care for Mom—a lot more than my father ever did, the lazy bastard."

"Isn't your father dead?" I asked.

She nodded slowly and a small grimace came to her face. "Heart attack in the middle of the night. I hope the son of a bitch suffered."

Okay, she is really out there. I slowly scooted away from her.

"Hey, what are you doing tonight?" she asked.

"Nothing in particular."

"Be ready at about seven o'clock. I'll come and pick you up."

"Where are we going?"

She smiled. "Where else? To spy on Deke and Abby."

CHAPTER 13

"Are you sure this is a good idea? What if he sees us?" My wild hair was like a neon sign, attracting all eyes to me. "If you hadn't noticed, I kinda stick out."

"You worry too much," Sheila said as she parked in the movie theater lot. "If they see us, we'll come up with something."

"Easy for you to say. I'm the one he'll curse out."

"I thought you said he didn't curse."

"He will if he finds out what I'm up to."

We stepped out of the car and proceeded to the ticket booth. All the while, I kept looking for Deke and Abby. If they weren't here yet, I knew they would show up soon. It wasn't like there was another movie theater they could go to. The town only had one.

"Look who's here," Sheila said as we neared the booth. She pointed to Marcus in the line. Just then, he looked up and saw us. He elbowed the guy behind him and they walked over to us.

"Hi, Maxine, Sheila," Marcus said. The corners of his lips turned up slightly as he looked at me. "This is my friend, Kent."

I nodded at Kent. He was a scruffy looking white boy, with dirty blonde hair and blue eyes. A gold hoop earring hung from his left earlobe.

"What are y'all doing here?" Marcus continued.

Sheila rolled her eyes. "Take a guess, idiot."

Marcus scowled at her. "I didn't know bats came out in the daytime." He shook his head. "Why'd you come here with her, Maxine? Spending time with the socially retarded?"

Sheila gave off a dry laugh. "Very funny. Now, are y'all paying our way or not?"

Kent looked like he was going to choke. "What? Pay for *you*?"

"I can't speak for you, Kent, but I'd be happy to pay for Maxine," Marcus said.

Sheila winked at Kent. "Well, blondie, that leaves you and me. What type of popcorn do you want?"

Kent groaned and followed Marcus back into line. As soon as they were out of range, Sheila grabbed my arm.

"Looks like this is your lucky day. You get to spy on Deke and be with Marcus at the same time. And speaking of Deke...."

I turned around as she began to trail off. Deke and Abby were making their way toward the booth. Abby noticed us and froze. She whispered something in Deke's ear, and his gaze locked in on us. Even from that far away, I could see the frown on his face. He tightened his grip around Abby's waist and walked to us.

Deke bored into me with an icy gaze. "I didn't expect to see you here," he said, through clenched teeth.

"We're doing that whole step-sister bonding thing," I said.

"Y'all would make perfect sisters," Abby said. "Both of you are lunatics."

"Takes one to know one," I whispered under my breath.

"Well, me and my date are going inside." Abby flashed a smile at us. "Too bad y'all don't have dates."

"But we do," I said, nodding back toward Marcus and Kent.

"You're here with Marcus?" Deke said. His eyes narrowed as Marcus and Kent walked back to us.

"Hi there, Daniel—"

"It's Deke."

Marcus wrapped his arm around me. Although his hand was a little close to my chest, I didn't stop him. "Sorry, Deke," he said. "I didn't know you guys were coming out here."

He shrugged. "A new movie attracts all types of people."

"You're right about that," I said, thinking about Abby.

"I don't know about y'all, but I'm hot as a dog in heat," Sheila said, fanning herself. "Y'all can stand out here if you all want to, but me and Kent are going inside."

"But—" Kent began.

"Come on, boy," she said as she grabbed his hand and pulled him behind her. "Behave, and I might let you kiss me good-night."

We followed them into the theater and found some seats. I sat with Deke on one side of me and Marcus on the other side. One guy seemed to want nothing to do with me, while the other guy couldn't keep his hands off me.

I took Marcus's hand from my leg and placed it in his lap. "I'm going to get some popcorn." I squeezed by Deke and Abby, and tapped Sheila on the arm. "I'm going to get some popcorn."

She nodded. "Okay."

I tapped her a little harder. "Don't you want some?"

She shook her head. "No, it gets stuck in my braces."

This time, I didn't waste time with the small nudges—I punched her in the shoulder. "I think you *do* want some popcorn."

"I do?"

"Yes, you do."

She cursed under her breath as she followed me out of the theater. I walked past the concession stand and was almost out the door when she grabbed my arm and pulled me back inside.

"And just where are you going?" she asked.

"Anywhere but here. I can't sit though a movie with Marcus on one side and Deke on the other. It's insane."

"And so are you." She turned me around and strong-armed me to the concession stand. "Don't forget why we're here. To spy on Deke and Abby. How would you feel if Deke and Abby got serious? What if they got married?" She shook her head. "And I don't want to even talk about kids."

I sighed. Just a couple of hours, I thought. That was all I'd have to sit through.

I nodded back at Sheila. "Okay, but don't hold me responsible if I kill her."

"Just don't get blood on my car seat."

I stretched as we walked out of the theater. That had to be the worse movie theater I had ever been in. I would probably have back spasms for the rest of my life from sitting in those seats. And my TV at home looked bigger than the screen. Sounded better too. I guess surround sound to them amounted to the little stereo speaker in the corner.

"What did you think about the movie?" Marcus asked.

I shrugged. I really didn't know what to think about the movie. I had been too busy with other issues to pay attention to it. Either I was watching Deke and Abby cuddle in their seats or I was fending off Marcus's roaming hands. I swear, every time he could, he put his hands on my thigh. I don't remember him actually eating any popcorn; his hands just seemed to cycle from the bucket to my leg. With all the butter and salt he left on my skin, it looked like a glazed ham.

"Marcus, over here," someone yelled.

A group of teenagers were assembled in the parking lot. They looked like living mannequins with all of the name-brand clothing they were wearing. I had never seen such an assortment of high priced jeans and t-shirts.

Marcus ambled over to the group, followed by Abby. I was amazed at the way the teenagers competed for Marcus and Abby's attention. It was as if a spotlight had zeroed in on them. They were the unquestionable center of attention of the group.

Out of the corner of my eye, I saw Deke exit the movie theater. Instead of walking to me, he went to Abby and Marcus and the group of teenagers. Deke looked totally at ease surrounded by the "in crowd." He was popular in his own right in high school. Deke wasn't the starting quarterback or the class president or anything like that. He was just a guy everyone liked. He was smart, but he never made anyone feel stupid. He could somehow make people feel better about themselves by just being around. Of course, I'm sure his resemblance to an Olympic Gold Medallist had nothing to do with his popularity.

Deke and Abby pulled away from the crowd and left the theater. A few minutes later, Marcus made his way over to me.

"What happened to you?" he asked. "I was looking for you."

"Umph," I said. "I was right here where you left me. I guess all those girls must have been blocking me from your view."

Marcus smiled that wonderful smile of his. "Please," he began, "those girls don't mean anything. They're just friends."

I rolled my eyes. This town seemed to have a very liberal definition for the word *friend*.

Marcus leaned over to my ear. His cologne wafted into my nostrils. The scent was what I thought sex would smell like.

"They're just jealous," he continued. "Let me make it up to you. The night is still young and there's so much more we could do."

"We?" I said. "As in you, me, Sheila, and Kent? Or we as in you, me, and little Marcus."

Marcus grabbed his crotch. "Which would you prefer?"

I burst out laughing. Marcus had to think he was the smoothest brother on the planet. Before I realized it, my gaze fell to his crotch.

Maybe "little Marcus" wasn't so little after all.

I could feel the pack of girls' eyes burying into me as I talked to him. I could almost read their minds. *Who is that nappy-headed, flat-chested, plain-Jane looking freak talking to Marcus?* they had to be thinking. If I were them, I'd be thinking the same thing.

"So what's the deal," Marcus said. "We gonna hook up tonight or not?"

"No, I'm going home," I said. "But ask me again tomorrow. Maybe we could have dinner or something."

"Or something?"

"Yeah, something," I whispered. Deke wasn't the only one who could have a summer fling.

I clutched at Marcus's shirt and pulled him even closer to me. We kissed, long and hard. This kiss was even stronger than the one at the picnic. Of course, a lot of it probably had to do with the three hot dogs with relish he ate during the movie.

His hands slipped from the small of my back to my butt. It was then that I stopped. I wasn't about to put on a porno in the parking lot.

He kissed my eyebrows, first the left, then the right. "That's not the only pair of things I want to kiss," he said.

I kissed him quickly once more, before walking away. "See you tomorrow," I said.

Sheila stared at me while I got into the car. I tried to ignore her glare, but finally I had to say something.

"What are you staring at?"

She laughed. "You're glowing. You probably had an orgasm right here in the parking lot."

I frowned. "I did not." I was a little hot, though. Hot and definitely bothered.

She started the car and pulled out of the lot. "You want to sleep with him, don't you?"

I shook my head. "No, of course not."

We rode in silence for all of ten seconds.

"Okay, maybe I do," I blurted out. "I mean, look at him. He is fine. *Fine!* Anyway, I'm eighteen years old, about to go to college. It's about time that I lose my virginity."

"So, you're going to do it?"

"I didn't say that."

"So, you aren't?"

"I didn't say that either."

She stopped the car and looked at me. "Then what are you saying?"

"I don't know," I said, burying my head in my hands. "I mean, on one hand, he's a slut. I know he is. But, he is so fine."

"You should hear what they say about him in the girls' bathroom at school," she said. "From the way they talk, he should charge girls admission to his privates."

"What's up with you and Kent?"

"Nothing at all," she said. "That boy is stiffer than stale bread. We kissed, though."

"Y'all kissed each other, or you kissed him?"

"Well, I kissed him. But he wanted to kiss me, I could tell." Sheila pulled up to a stoplight. "I wonder what it feels like."

"What?"

"Sex. I wonder what sex feels like."

I shrugged. "I don't know. It's not like I go around having it every day." In truth, the entirety of my sexual experience consisted of a few passionate kisses and some wild groping, and that was almost two years ago. I had never even seen a guy naked. Of course, slow dancing with some over anxious, pimple-faced pervert with excessively thin slacks more than made up for that.

"I think I've had enough excitement for one day," I said. "I'm ready to go home and take a long, hot bath."

"Not yet," Sheila said. "We're still not finished with Deke and Abby."

I sat up. "What do you mean?"

As she continued driving, she poked around underneath her seat with her free hand, and finally pulled out a walkie-talkie.

I shook my head. "I don't understand. I don't think Abby is going to relay messages to us while she's swapping spit with Deke."

"Don't you have any imagination?" she asked. "I have a friend that's good with electronics. He rigged the other walkie-talkie so that it's constantly on. All I have to do is get close enough to pick up the signal, and we can listen in. All we may hear is groans, but that's a different story."

"What are you, a spy?" I replied. "And just how do you plan to get the other walkie-talkie close enough to Deke and Abby?"

A mischievous grin came to her face. "Don't worry about that," she said. "During the movie, I had another friend slip it in his car."

"Wait a minute. Deke is extremely protective of his car. He always locks his doors."

Sheila coughed. "My friend is an…escape artist, of sorts. He's good at getting in and out of places, and making things disappear."

"You mean he's a thief," I said. "Suppose all of this works. What happens if they find the walkie-talkie?"

Sheila smiled. "Deny, deny, deny."

Sheila turned off the lights and crept down the road. We had passed by a pond moments before and had spotted Deke's car there.

"Okay, we're going to have to get a lot closer before we're in range," she said as she grabbed the walkie-talkie and stepped out of the car. I followed her down the road.

The sky was pitch black, save for a few stars dotting the sky. The odor of manure clogged the air. We kicked up small clouds of dust as we crept toward the car.

We camped out about twenty feet away, behind a small grove. I peered into Deke's car, but couldn't distinguish between him and Abby. They were so close they looked like some continuous blob.

Sheila turned on the walkie-talkie. It crackled and hissed as we tried to make out what they were saying.

At first, I couldn't tell what was going on. The walkie-talkie was alive with a smorgasbord of sounds. Then I heard it.

"Ohhh."

What was going on in there?

That one moan was followed by a barrage of others. I peeked through the trees to try and get a better look, but I still couldn't see anything. After listening to more of the sounds they were making, maybe it was for the best that I couldn't see anything.

"Is that how it sounds?" Sheila asked. "Where are all the love grunts?"

Love grunts? "Sheila, please."

But then I heard what could only be "love grunts." I was getting more and more irritated by the minute. Well, actually by the second.

"Why are you so mad?" Sheila asked.

"Mad?" I snapped. "What makes you think I'm mad?"

"For starters, you're yelling," she said. She looked at my hands. "And, you're choking the life out of that branch."

I released the tree branch and wiped my hands against my shorts. Maybe I was mad? But mad about what? Mad because Abby was so…liberated, or because she was so liberated with Deke.

I hit myself on the forehead. I should be happy for Deke, right? This was what he wanted. Maybe Abby was the one for him. But who was the one for me? Marcus?

I closed my eyes and tried to imagine Marcus and myself. I wondered if he could make me utter the same sounds that I was hearing over the walkie-talkie.

"Maxine," Sheila hissed. "Are you paying attention?"

My eyes flashed open. "What are you talking about?"

"Shhh," she said. "Listen."

I tuned out the crickets and the frogs, and focused on the walkie-talkie.

"I'm not good enough for you? Is that it?" a voice from the walkie-talkie said. It was Abby's voice.

"No, it's not that, and you know it," Deke said. "I'm just not ready."

"You don't get much readier than that," Abby said. "That's about as hard as it gets."

Sheila immediately clamped her hand over her mouth so she wouldn't laugh. I personally didn't see anything funny.

"Is it because I'm white?"

"No, no, of course it's not that. I'm just uncomfortable."

There was a long pause on the other end.

"It's because of her, isn't it?" Abby said.

"It's just…," Deke began, before trailing off.

"You love her, don't you?" Abby said. "After all the shit she's put you through, you still love her."

There was another pause. I didn't know if Deke was being silent or if he was shaking his head yes or no.

"What the hell is wrong with you?" Abby yelled. "Can't you see that she doesn't want you? She's too selfish to be worried about anyone's feelings but her own."

Sheila frowned. "Who is she talking about?"

"I don't know," I said. "I think she's talking about Yvonne, Deke's ex-girlfriend."

"What do you mean, 'You don't know?'" Sheila said. "I thought you and Deke were best friends. Don't y'all talk about stuff like this?"

I shrugged. "Deke can be very private about his love life sometimes."

Sheila's mouth dropped open. "Maxine, don't you see—"

Abby's voice crackled through the walkie-talkie, interrupting Sheila. "Tell me the truth," she said. "Do you still love her?"

Before Deke could respond, Sheila reached over and turned off the walkie-talkie.

I jumped up. "What the—"

"We can't do this."

"Why not? Just a few minutes ago, you were gung-ho about it. Now you're backing out?"

"Believe me, there are some things you don't want to hear over a walkie-talkie."

"But—"

"Come on," Sheila said. "Mom will bitch all night if I get home too late."

I shook my head. There was no use in arguing, because Sheila had already begun walking back to the car. I gave a fleeting glance back, before I got up and followed her.

CHAPTER 14

I sat in the living room, waiting in the dark. Why I chose to sit in the dark, I didn't know. Maybe I thought things would seem less complicated if I sat in darkness; that would be one less of the five senses to deal with.

Did Deke do it? Did he have sex with her? I didn't actually think he did, but I wasn't completely sure. They obviously had some type of bond, being that he shared things with her he didn't share with me.

I hoped he didn't do it, but I didn't know why. Why was it okay for me to lose my virginity, but not okay for Deke? Why did I hate Abby so much? She hadn't done anything to me. Deke liked her and that should have been enough for me. But for some reason, it wasn't.

And what were he and Abby talking about? I didn't know what was worse: him sleeping with Abby, or him keeping secrets from me. What type of friendship did we have if he had to confide in a stranger instead of his best friend?

Seconds, minutes, hours passed before I heard a car pull in the yard. The back door opened and shut, and someone, presumably Deke, began walking down the hallway.

"Deke," I called out. My voice was a soft whine. I had wanted to speak louder, to sound surer of myself, but a whisper was all I could muster.

He appeared in the doorway. "Were you waiting up for me?"

"Yes…and no. I couldn't sleep."

"I can hardly see you," he said. He reached out for the light switch. "Let me turn on—"

"No. No lights."

Deke nodded and walked into the room. He sat on the couch, but not really beside me. The distance between us was a few inches at the most, but it felt like miles. I tried to block out the smell of Abby's perfume on his body. It was sickeningly sweet and seemed to reek from his every pore.

"How was your date?" I asked.

"I've had better," he replied. "It's probably safe to say that Abby and I aren't going out anymore."

"Oh."

"Is that it?" he asked. I could hear the frown in his voice. "I thought you'd be happier."

Earlier that night, I would have been happier if he had told me news like that. Ecstatic, even. Now, I wasn't sure. I felt hurt that Deke had revealed some deep, dark secret to Abby that he couldn't tell me. Some best friend.

"What about your date?" he continued. "You seemed to enjoy yourself."

"It wasn't much of a date. It was more Sheila's idea than mine."

"Are you and Marcus going out again?"

I swiftly nodded. "Tomorrow night."

Silence echoed in the room.

If I hadn't seen Deke walk into the room, I would have thought he was a statue. His breaths came so slowly and quietly, they were almost non-existent.

"That's great, I guess," he said. He gave off a nervous, spotty laugh. "Maybe Marcus isn't so bad. Abby speaks highly of him. She seems to think y'all make a good couple."

Abby, taking up for me? What was the world coming to?

"Maybe I should cancel," I said. I didn't think my brain was quite ready for what my body was yearning to do. I wondered if I could go through with it. Could I really sleep with Marcus?

Deke sat up, and even though I couldn't see his eyes, I knew he was staring at me. "Why are you thinking about canceling? I thought you liked him."

"I do, but—"

"But, nothing. It won't hurt to at least go out with him. I'm always saying you don't go out enough." He scooted over to me. "You're going on this date, if I have to handcuff you to Marcus's arm."

I laughed. "He would probably like that. I think his testosterone level is stuck somewhere in overdrive."

He patted me on the knee. "Then it's settled. Tomorrow, you'll go out with Marcus. You don't need a chaperone, do you?"

I laughed again. "I'm a big girl; I think I can take care of myself." I paused. "You want me to hook you up with Sheila? I'm sure she's free."

"I think I'll pass," he said. "I'm going to take a break from females for a while."

"How long is a while?"

"About thirty years."

"Yeah, right." I let both of our laughs die down.

"What about Yvonne?" I asked.

"What about her?" he said. "It's over."

"I thought you and Yvonne would be together forever."

He shook his head. "I never thought that."

"Then why did you stay with her for so long?"

He shrugged.

"Maybe you should have slept with her."

"Very funny."

"I'm serious, Deke," I said. "Think about it. We'll be college freshmen in the fall." I paused. "I think I'm ready to...."

He jerked up. "You think you're ready to do what?"

I dropped my gaze to my lap. "Nothing," I murmured.

Deke was silent for a few moments, before spitting out his thoughts. "You plan on sleeping with him, don't you?"

Deke's tone of voice made me feel dirty inside. He made me sound like a prostitute for just entertaining the idea of sex with Marcus. He didn't have the right to talk to me like that, being as he may have just had sex himself.

I crossed my arms. "Don't you think it's about time? I'm eighteen."

"Time? Jesus Christ, losing your virginity isn't a rite of passage. You hardly know the boy."

"You don't have any room to criticize," I snapped. "You've known Abby for less than a week and you two are already exchanging bodily fluids." I stared at Deke. "I know y'all did more than talk after the movie." I could feel myself shaking. "You *fucked* her, didn't you!"

I was sorry before the words were even out of my mouth. Of all the curse words in the world, that was the one that Deke hated the most. It was a vile and cruel word, and he felt that it didn't belong in anyone's vocabulary. I had never said it to his face before, until tonight.

"I didn't mean it like that," I began. "What I meant—"

"What Abby and I did," Deke said, "is private, and none of your business."

My soul felt like it sank beneath the cushions of the couch as his response echoed in my mind. Plain and simple, I was losing my best friend.

"Keep your damn secret, I don't care what you did." I could feel my voice rising, but I didn't care. "And while I'm at it, I don't care what you think. I'm a grown woman, and I can sleep with whomever I want."

We sat in silence for countless minutes. I almost wished I could turn off all the images flashing through my head, but I was afraid of the emptiness I would be left with if that happened.

"Maybe I should go to bed," Deke said as he began to get up.

I placed my hand on his knee, signaling him to stop. I couldn't let the night end like this. "Do you want to talk about anything?" I asked.

His eyes seemed to open up to me for a moment. "I...I can't," he stammered. "You wouldn't understand."

"What's wrong? I feel like there's this invisible wall between us. I can see you, but I can't reach you."

Deke was quiet for a few seconds.

"We all have our secrets, Maxine."

"No! Everyone else has secrets. Not us. Not Deke and Maxine."

"We can't be Deke and Maxine forever."

"What does that mean?"

Deke didn't answer me. Instead, he stood from the couch. "I'm really tired, and I need to get my thoughts together. We'll talk tomorrow."

"But what about—"

"I promise," he said. "Tomorrow."

He walked to the doorway. But before leaving, he stopped and looked back.

"Maxine," he whispered. "Do you really plan on sleeping with him?"

The sound of Deke's voice startled me. His words seemed to float across the room, drenched in a strange kind of sadness.

The sheer power of his question made me turn away from him. I didn't know what to say, much less how to say it.

Finally, I summoned the courage to look at him. "Deke, I—"

I stopped and sighed. I was talking to an empty room.

CHAPTER 15

"I can't believe my baby girl is actually going on a date," Jack said as he took his millionth picture of me.

"I *am* eighteen," I said as Jack pushed me into another pose. "And why are you taking so many pictures? It's not like I'm getting married."

Jack finally put the camera down. "I know this isn't an important day for you, but it is for me. I've never had a chance to do this before."

"To do what?"

He smiled. "You know…to be a father."

"Does this mean you're going to give Marcus the third degree when he comes to pick me up?"

"Of course," Jack replied. "Isn't that what all fathers are supposed to do?"

Jack paced across the kitchen floor. Every five minutes, he'd push aside the curtains and peer out the window. He seemed so nervous, you'd think he was the one going on the date. I was plenty nervous myself. Little did Jack know, tonight was just as important to me as it was to him. I could already feel Marcus's hands and lips all over me, as he peeled my clothes off.

"What do you think of Marcus," I asked as Jack spied through the window once more. "He's a nice guy, isn't he?"

Jack nodded. "He's a great kid. Always active in church activities…he's good husband material."

"Jack…."

"I'm not trying to marry you off. I'm just making an observation, that's all."

I laughed. Today had been a perfect day so far. It was the first day since being here that Jack and I hadn't argued. Things were beginning to feel normal—or as normal as our situation could be. As much as Jack didn't know how to be a father to me, I didn't know how to be a daughter to him. But we were figuring it out together, and that was okay.

"Now Maxine, I'm not going to give you a big speech," Jack said. "You know right from wrong. I know I can trust you to stay out of trouble."

I tried to bury my thoughts of sex with Marcus, as if Jack could read my mind. "Don't worry," I said. "I won't do anything I shouldn't."

Jack seemed satisfied with that answer. He gave me a quick hug and returned to his vigil at the window. "It looks like your carriage has arrived," Jack said. "Marcus just pulled up."

"I'm going to get my purse," I said. "Can you let him in?"

Jack nodded. "Take your time," he said. "This will give me and Marcus a chance to have a little chat."

I rolled my eyes and headed to my room. As I grabbed my purse and turned around to leave, I almost bumped into Deke. He stood in my doorway, saying nothing, just looking at me with tired, melancholy eyes.

"Hey, stranger," I said as I punched his shoulder, in an attempt to lighten the atmosphere. "I didn't know you were home."

"Marcus and I pulled up at the same time."

Deke had been gone most of the day. For all I knew, he could have been curled up with Abby.

"Are you ready?" he asked.

I forced myself to nod. I knew he wasn't asking about the date itself. "As ready as I've ever been." I slung my purse over my shoulder. "I hope you're not planning to try to talk me out of this."

"I know you better than that," he said. "Arguing with you is like arguing with a brick wall; some things don't budge."

"Thanks, I think," I said. I glanced at my watch. "Listen, Marcus is waiting on me…."

"Just so you know, last night, Abby and I—"

"Deke, stop," I said. "You don't have to tell me anything. It's none of my business."

"I know," he said. "But I still want you to know, Abby and I did-n't have sex."

I frowned on the outside, but on the inside I heaved a sigh of relief. "Why not? Didn't you want to?"

Deke flashed me a half-smile. "Yes, I wanted to. I really, really wanted to. But I changed my mind." He began retreating down the hallway. "There are some things that you want more than sex."

"What does that mean?"

Deke was almost out of sight. "It doesn't really matter anymore," he said. And then he was gone.

I swear, Deke made me want to strangle him sometimes. He was like a jigsaw puzzle that was missing half of its pieces. I ran after him, determined to finish this cryptic conversation. Just as I was about to knock on his bedroom door, Jack appeared.

"What's taking so long?" Jack asked. "Aren't you ready?"

I stared at Deke's door, willing myself to knock on it. But instead, I let my hand fall to my side.

"Yeah, I'm ready."

I hope.

As I sat across from Marcus in our restaurant booth, I had to con-stantly remind myself to stop beaming. Marcus looked like a human version of an ice cream sundae. Sweet to the taste and covered in choco-late. Of course, I conveniently chose to forget that too much chocolate was bad for you.

"You look fine as hell," he said as his gaze darted across my body. He licked his lips with his wicked tongue and smiled at me. I could feel myself blushing. Rarely did someone call me pretty, much less fine. As far as I was concerned, we could push the food off the table and get started right now.

"Your friend, Kent, didn't seem to care for Sheila that much," I said between bites of my salad. "Did he say anything about her?"

"Only that he thought she was the craziest girl he ever met. You know she was committed once."

"Committed? As in to an asylum?"

"Yep. Right after her father died." He leaned closer to me. "Some say that she may have killed him."

I frowned. "I thought he died of a heart attack."

"Is that what she told you? The sheriff found her father behind a dumpster, with two gunshot shells in his back. Never did find the weapon, though."

"Why would she want to kill him?"

He shrugged. "The dumb bitch is crazy, that's why. Her pop was a big man in the community. Was on the city council and everything. Everybody liked him."

"Apparently not the person who killed him," I said. I made a mental note to talk to Deke about this later. I could deal with one murderer in the family, but two was pushing it.

"I can't eat another bite," I said as I dropped my napkin in my plate. Boy, was that a lie. I could feel my stomach gurgling, waiting for more food to drop down the shoot. I had tried to be "ladylike" and had only ordered a salad. What I was really yearning for was a half rack of baby back ribs, not some soggy lettuce.

I carefully patted my hair and straightened my blouse. Sheila and I had gone on a frenzied shopping spree earlier that day to find something suitable for tonight. We finally settled on a simple, scarlet red blouse and a denim skirt. Sheila also stressed that I wear no stockings, for "easy access," as she liked to call it. She tried to convince me to go without underwear as well, but that was where I had to draw the line. I looked down at my purse; it too was Sheila's idea. She made it a point to stuff a box of condoms in it, right between my pepper spray and pocketknife.

The waitress came back to the table and slid the bill to Marcus. Marcus ogled at her like she was an entree on the menu. I could just imagine what he was thinking: *Yeah, I'll take two orders of tits, with your thighs on the side.*

I felt a pang of jealousy as he watched her sashay to another table. He opened the bill and whistled.

I reached for my purse. "You paid for the movie yesterday; let me pick this up."

"Okay," he said as he slid the bill toward me.

What the…? He could have at least taken a breath before he agreed. Whatever happened to chivalry? Or good manners for that matter?

I looked at the bill. I saw what Marcus had whistled about—it was almost forty dollars. And my salad only cost six. So not only was I hungry, but thanks to Marcus's appetite, I was broke.

I dropped the money on the table and we left the restaurant. As soon as we were outside, he had his hands wrapped around my waist and his lips on my neck.

"Marcus, please. People are watching."

He let up from my neck just long enough to speak. "They're just jealous of us."

I smiled. Jealous of us. *Jealous of me.* That was an interesting concept. I had never thought of anyone being jealous of me before. No one ever had any reason to be jealous of me before. Not until tonight.

We finally made it to the car and left the restaurant. Marcus had the windows rolled down and the sunroof open, and was blasting rap music. The entire car was wired with speakers, causing me to vibrate with every downbeat.

"Where are we going?" I yelled over the noise.

"Somewhere special," he replied. "Just sit back and relax."

Relax? It wasn't easy to relax with blood spurting from my ears.

Finally, the song ended, and Marcus popped in another disc. This one was better than the first, but not by much. It was a slow, bass heavy song. I couldn't make out all of the words, but I think the singer said something about "slipping my firmness in you until your love juices flow." I wondered if that was meant to be sexy.

"There's an old pond out here that I go to when I need to be by myself," he said. "It's like my own private hideaway. No one else knows about it."

Marcus and I rode along the same streets Sheila and I had traveled the other night. He pulled into his "private hideaway," and parked in almost the same spot where Deke's car was yesterday.

"So now what?" I asked.

"Let's talk," he said as he stepped out of the car.

"Where are you going?"

He opened the back door and climbed in. "It's easier to talk in the back seat."

I burst out laughing. "Really? Well, I think I can talk just as easily up here." I knew exactly what he was up to, but I didn't want to look too anxious.

"Aww, come on Maxine," he whined. "I'm lonely back here by myself."

I sighed and finally got out of the car. I opened the door and climbed into the back seat. But before I even had a chance to shut the door, Marcus was on top of me.

He placed a few kisses along my neck. His body moved and grinded against mine.

"I thought you wanted to talk," I said.

He stared at me and licked his lips. "What, you want me to stop?"

Game time, Maxine. What are you going to do?

I pulled him closer to me. "We can talk later."

"Get out!"

"What?"

"Bitch, you heard me," Marcus said. He opened the door and shoved me out. "Get out of my goddamn car!"

I stumbled around and tried to gain my balance. This was a fine time for me to start wearing high-heeled sandals.

"Listen, asshole—"

"Shut up!" he yelled. "I should have known better than messing with an uppity white bitch." He shook his head. "Just because you're white, you think you're better than me, huh?"

"I'm not white!"

"Please, you're whiter than two week old dog shit!" He flung my purse at me. "All you white bitches are alike. Wanna piece of nigger dick."

I stared at Marcus. I didn't know what to say. I looked down at myself. My grass-stained knees were shaking like trees in a hurricane. I noticed my half open blouse. I tried to close it, but my hands were trembling too much to line up the buttons. As I fumbled with my clothes, Marcus started his car.

"Where are you going? I know you aren't gonna leave me out here!"

He sneered at me. "You gonna let me fuck?"

I balled my fist up and fiercely shook my head.

"Well, you can stay your white ass out here." He squealed off and disappeared into the night.

CHAPTER 16

"Okay, what happened?" Sheila asked as we pulled out of the parking lot.

I buried my head in my hands. "Sheila, not now." Even though it was the middle of summer, I was shivering like I was buried in ice.

"Oh, no you don't. I'm missing Baywatch, coming out here picking you up. And you know how good David Hasselhoff looks in swim trunks."

I had to smile at that one. I sighed and lifted my head back up. "What do you want to know?"

"For starters, why am I picking you up outside of Efram's Tackle Shop?"

"Going fishing?"

"Cute," she replied. "What happened to Marcus?"

The sound of his name made me want to throw up. "He kicked me out of the car and left me at the pond."

"He did what! That no good, back-stabbing, little dick—well, maybe not little dick—two timing, cold sore giving bastard!" Sheila was so busy waiving her finger in the air I thought she was going to run off the road.

"I guess I would have been pissed off too, if I was expecting to get something and came up empty handed."

Sheila looked at me like I was crazy. "Girl, I know you ain't rationalizing this shit. That's why God gave him hands. If Marcus wanted sex that bad, he could have done it himself. That still gave him no right to leave you stranded."

Sheila ran through a red light. "That's why I hate men sometimes. They think their way is the only way. Then, they get mad when someone tells them otherwise."

While Sheila continued to rant, I replayed the entire night over in my mind. I had never seen someone so vicious before. The crazy thing was, I had been black for eighteen years, and had never been called a nigger, coon, or anything else remotely derogatory, at least not to my face. It took me being part white to get racial slurs yelled at me.

"Why did you change your mind about sleeping with him?" she asked.

I shrugged. "It just didn't feel right."

"That's a good enough reason for me," she said. She pulled into my driveway. "Do you want me to come in for a while?"

"No, but thanks." I started to get out of the car, but she grabbed my arm.

"Tomorrow, we're going out. Just the two of us."

I shook my head. "I don't know...."

She rolled her eyes. "Stop making excuses. You need this, whether you want to admit it or not."

I nodded. "See you tomorrow," I said, and stepped out of the car.

I watched as Sheila pulled out of the yard. You know, I could actually see her as my sister. I had never had anything close to a sister before. It was a nice feeling.

I moped to the front door and fished my keys out of my purse. I was hoping everyone would be asleep when I got home. Of course, things never went as planned where I was concerned.

I straightened my hair and made sure all of my clothes were arranged the correct way. Luckily, I had managed to get most of the dirt and mud off my clothes and skin. I brushed the last pieces of grass from my sleeves and tried to scrape the mud from my sandals.

I walked into the house and was surprised to see Jack sitting at the table. "What are you still doing up?" I asked as I entered the kitchen. "I figured everyone would be in bed by now."

"Just working on some figures for the church," he said. He looked at me, with bloodshot eyes and heavy, sagging eyelids.

"Don't you have to be up in a few hours?" I asked. "You should be in bed."

He waved me off. "I just have a few more things I need to look over," he said. He smiled at me. "Did you enjoy yourself tonight?"

"As much as I enjoy Sunday morning service."

Jack frowned. "You and Marcus didn't hit it off?"

"Nope." I tried to laugh to myself, but as I stared at Jack's red hair and pale skin, everything Marcus said flashed back.

White bitch. White bitch.

"Maxine, what's wrong? You're zoning out."

I shook my head. "I'm just tired." I sat at the table and stared at him. Jack Phillips. My father. My dad. I looked at his eyes. They were gray, like mine. But they looked old. Old and tired.

"Do you—we—have any other family around here? Cousins or nephews or anything like that?"

Jack rubbed at the stubble on his face. "What makes you ask that?"

"I don't know," I said. "I just wanted to know if there was anyone else around here that looked kinda like me. It'd be nice to have a big family."

It'd be nice to fit in somewhere.

Jack shook his head. "I was an only child."

"What about your mother? Tell me about her."

Jack's eyes lit up, the same as they had when I first heard him talk about her. "She was extremely beautiful. She had long, flowing red hair. Even though she grew up on a farm, her hands weren't rough or calloused. They were so smooth, so soft."

As Jack continued to describe his mother—my grandmother—I could almost see her standing in front of me. She was short and petite, but that didn't mean she was a pushover. Her own mother had died when she was young, so she was forced to care for her younger siblings.

"What about your father?"

"He's dead."

"That's it?" I asked. After everything he said about his mother, I was expecting a little more.

"Yes," he mumbled. "That's it."

Jack stared at me for some uneasy seconds, before a yawn broke his gaze.

"I refuse to let you stay up any longer." I leaned over and closed his notebook. "Jack, this can wait until tomorrow."

"But—"

"Who's in charge around here, me or you?"

I watched as he slowly rose from his chair. "Is Deke in his room?" I asked.

Jack nodded. "He should be. He's been here all night." Jack began to walk out of the room, but turned back around.

"I'm jealous," he said.

I frowned. "What are you talking about?"

Jack sank back into his seat. "I'm jealous of Deke, of the relation-ship he has with you. The relationship *I* should have had with you." Jack laughed. "I'm a grown man and I'm jealous of a kid."

"Hey, there's enough of me to go around." I paused and thought about what I said. "Maybe that didn't come out right...."

Jack placed his hand on mine. "I understand exactly what you're trying to say." He stood up and kissed me on the forehead. "Good night, Maxine. And thanks."

Jack's entire body seemed to creak as he made his way down the hallway. I wished he didn't look so sad. Was that what I had to look forward to when I got to his age?

I tried to forget about the night's fiasco as I got ready for bed. And I was doing pretty well until I went to take a shower. One look in the bathroom mirror, and it all came rushing back.

I stood in the shower, pale and naked, and scrubbed my body. But no matter how hard I scrubbed I could still feel his hands on me. No matter how hot the water flowed, it couldn't burn off the trace of his lips against my skin. I couldn't believe that just yesterday, I had dreamed of Marcus's hands and lips traveling all over me.

I turned off the water and stood in the shower for a few moments. Part of me hoped that my whiteness would disappear down the drain with the rest of the dirt and muck.

Finally, I stepped out. I wiped the fog off the mirror and stared at myself again. My skin looked so pale. My hair looked so red.

I rubbed at my face. Maybe I was trying to erase the feel of his mouth, or maybe I was trying to wipe away the color of my skin. I really didn't know. But I rubbed and scratched and clawed until my hands were tired and my face was red and my skin felt raw. I gazed into the mirror again.

Still white.

I slipped into my nightclothes and returned to my room. I opened the door to find Deke sitting on my bed.

"I figured you'd want to talk," he said.

I just shrugged and sat beside him.

"What happened tonight?" he asked. "Did you and Marcus…"

"No."

"Why not?"

"I didn't want to."

"But yesterday—"

"Yesterday was yesterday," I said. "You changed your mind. Why can't I?"

Deke seemed taken aback. "Of course you can." He took my face in his hands and tilted it toward the light. "Why are you so red? Did he hurt you?"

I shook my head.

"Then why—"

"I don't want to talk about this anymore." I jumped off the bed and walked to the window. A full moon hung in the sky.

A full, white moon.

The bed creaked and I heard light footsteps behind me. I don't know why, but I felt myself trembling.

Deke placed one hand lightly on my waist and the other on my shoulder. Instantly, I stopped shaking. His touch wasn't heavy and overbearing, like Marcus's. Rather, it was a soft, subtle touch, like a warm fleece blanket on a cold night.

I turned around and stared at him. Deke's gaze was as soft as his hands.

"Why doesn't anyone want me?" I finally said. "Why can't people accept me for me?"

Deke wrapped his arms around me as if he was trying to shield me from all of the hurt I felt. "Maxine, you have a family, a full family. You have a mother, a father, even a new sister. And, you have me. We all love you very much, just like you are."

He placed a small kiss on my forehead, right where Jack had placed one earlier. "I know you don't want to hear this, but God will always be there for you. I know you have your own beliefs, but I sincerely believe God is helping you. He has provided you with all of these people now, when you need them the most. And somewhere, deep inside, I know you believe that, too."

I kept my head buried in his chest. He made me feel so safe, I didn't want to let go.

I finally looked up at him. "Will you stay with me tonight?"

His mouth dropped slightly open, then he nodded.

"You're my best friend; of course I'll stay."

I woke up to the smell of bacon frying. Well, more like bacon burning. I rolled out of bed and grabbed my watch. It was almost noon.

I walked down the hall and peeked into the kitchen. Deke was running back and forth from the counter to the stove, with a cookbook in one hand and a large wooden spoon in the other. The way flour covered his face you'd have thought he'd been swimming in it. And I didn't know why he had an apron on. He had more food on his clothes and the floor than on the apron. He ran back to the refrigerator, and almost slipped on an egg yoke.

"Good morning," I said, louder than necessary as I made my entrance.

Deke slammed the door shut and spun around. This time he did slip.

"Are you okay?" I asked as I rushed to him. I side-stepped the egg yoke and helped him to his feet.

"Who knew cooking was so hard," he said as he brushed himself off. In the process, he got flour and egg in his hair.

"Deke, you're a mess," I said. I reached around his waist and untied the apron. "Give me this and go take a shower."

"But—"

I slapped him on the arm, causing a mini flour storm. "Go!"

He obliged and trudged out of the room. By the time he returned, I had the kitchen cleaned up, had bacon, sausage and grits on the table, and was putting the finishing touches on the scrambled eggs.

I thought Deke was going to trip over his bottom lip, the way his mouth hung open. He stumbled over to me and stared at the stove.

"Deke, don't drool in the food."

He snapped his mouth shut. "Who cleaned up the kitchen?"

"The Jolly Green Giant." I rolled my eyes. "Who do you think?"

"You?"

"Did you come up with that all by yourself?" I scraped the last of the eggs onto a plate and brought it to the table.

"You cook, too?"

"Wow, I guess you really are college material." I sat down at the table. "Come on, let's eat."

Deke followed me to the table. "I didn't know you could cook."

"With Mom always gone, if I didn't cook for myself, I would have starved." I hurriedly heaped a pile of food on my plate and shoved a piece of bacon into my mouth.

"What about grace?"

"God will have to excuse me today," I said. "I'm a little too hungry to put up with His ritualistic butt-kissing ceremony."

Deke shot me a dirty look and bowed his head.

"Just what exactly are you praying for?" I asked after he began eating.

"Plenty of things. I've got a lot to be thankful for."

I licked the grease off my fingers. "Like what?"

"Like being alive, for instance. For waking up with no serious illnesses. For being able to eat such a wonderful meal." He flashed me a smile. "For having such a great friend."

It took me a second to realize he was talking about me. I turned from his gaze and tried to stop myself from blushing. "Please, I'm no great friend."

Deke laughed so hard, he began choking on his food. He wiped his eyes and cleared his throat.

"Are you serious? Look at all of your qualities."

"Yeah, right," I said. "I'm crass, sarcastic, rude—"

"Sweet, good-hearted, compassionate."

"I'm scrawny—"

"You're slim."

"I'm pale—"

"You're light toned."

I slammed my hand on the table. "Will you let me finish!" That boy was going to make me stab him with my fork.

"I have too much hair," I continued.

"Better to have too much than not enough."

"I'm ugly."

"You're the epitome of beauty."

I laughed. "You're not going to let me win, are you?"

"Nope."

"Don't you know you should always—what happened to you?" I rose and walked around the table to him. With the strong light in the kitchen, I was able to get a good look at his face. I could just see the traces of a purple bruise on his cheek. I placed my fingers on the bruise and he instantly pulled away. "Did you put any ice on it?" I asked.

"Nope. It wasn't a top priority."

I went to the sink and grabbed a dishtowel. I dropped some ice in it and ran it under the faucet for a second. "What do you mean, not a top priority?"

"What, you're a nurse, too?"

"Cook, nurse, maid. You name it, I can do it. Now stop trying to change the subject." I pulled a chair to him and placed the ice on his bruise. "Did you fall or something?"

"Or something."

"Maybe you don't remember, but I'm the sarcastic one here. What happened?"

Deke sighed. "You elbowed me."

"I did not."

He shook his head. "Believe me, you did."

"I don't remember—"

"You were asleep."

I removed the towel and stared at the bruise again. I pressed against it and Deke jerked away again.

"Do you have to do that? I've already been through enough physical abuse for one night."

"What? I did more?"

Deke rolled up his sleeve. Three long scratches were engraved into his skin.

"Did I do that?"

He nodded.

I went to the cabinet for some rubbing alcohol. "Why didn't you get up?"

"Like I said, the bruises weren't a priority."

I crossed my arms. "What was so important that you couldn't get up?"

Deke shrugged before cramming his mouth full with scrambled eggs.

I grabbed a few cotton balls and began swabbing the rubbing alcohol on his arm. The entire time, I could feel his gaze on me.

"Maxine, stop with the alcohol." He slid away from me and rolled down his sleeve. "We need to talk."

"If this is about my date, then—"

"This isn't about your date. This is about me."

Deke rose from his seat and began pacing the room. "Listen, I'm really nervous right now, so you'll have to excuse me."

I tried to look calm on the outside, but on the inside it felt like my heart was going to burst out of my chest.

By now, Deke was wrenching his hands together. "I don't know how to say this, but if I don't say it now, I never will."

I tried to give Deke a reassuring smile. "You can tell me anything."

Well, don't tell me you're gay.

Or that you slept with Abby.

Or that you found the walkie-talkie.

"Okay, here goes." Deke sucked in a deep breath. "I'm in love with—"

"I can't believe you went and fell in love with Abby! You hardly know her."

Deke's mouth dropped open. "What?"

"I mean, if you said you loved Yvonne, I could understand that. But Abby?"

"Maxine—"

"She wouldn't know real love if it jumped up and slapped her in the face."

"Maxine!"

I stopped ranting and looked at him. "Well, she wouldn't."

Deke shook his head. "She's not the only one."

I frowned. "What are you saying?"

"I'm saying that I don't love Abby. Or Yvonne."

I knew it. He was gay.

"It's you," he said. He dropped his hands by his sides. "Maxine, I'm in love with you."

"With…me?"

Oh.

My.

God.

"Maxine, open the door."

"I can't. I'm getting dressed."

I heard Deke sigh from the other side of the door. "You've been getting dressed for two hours."

"Perfection takes time."

Deke pounded on the door again. "We really need to talk about this."

"What's there to talk about? You said that you loved me. End of story."

"You running out of the room wasn't exactly the response I was looking for."

I jumped from the bed and marched across the room. I yanked the door open so hard, I thought it was going to fly off its hinges.

"And just what type of response *were* you looking for?"

"I don't know."

Deke stood in the hallway, his fists jammed in his pockets, staring at me with his deep, dark, rich—*what was I thinking?*

I turned and walked back toward the bed. "Are you gonna stand there all day, or are you coming in?"

I collapsed on the bed and stared at him. He stood a few feet away from me, with his hands still in his pockets. Now, his gaze was darting everywhere but on me.

"You're the one that wanted to talk," I said. "So talk."

He finally took one of his hands out of his pocket, to wipe at his face. "I hope I didn't surprise you too much."

"Tell that to my doctor once he sees my blood pressure." I picked at the lint on my bed. "Well, how long have…"

"I been in love with you?"

I nodded.

"I don't really know. A long time. Maybe too long." He smiled, seemingly more to himself than to me. "I didn't actually admit it to myself until about a year ago."

"A year ago? Why didn't you say anything before?"

He stepped closer. "If I had said something then, would your reaction have been any different?"

"Umph. I guess we'll never know."

Deke threw his hands up. "When I realized how I felt about you, I decided not to tell you."

"So you've been lying to me."

He shook his head. "No, not lying. Just being selective with my truths."

"In the real world, we call that lying."

He rolled his eyes. "Whether you want to admit it or not, you needed a friend back then. You always have. And like it or not, I was the only person around."

Deke walked over to the bed and sat beside me. "I knew things would change once I told you how I felt. So in order to save the friendship, I hid my feelings."

"Why do you always do that?" I lightly stroked the bruise on his face. "Why do you always put me ahead of you?"

He shrugged. "Because I love you."

"Love must make you stupid."

He nodded. "Believe me, it does."

"Why tell me now, after waiting so long?"

He chewed on his lip for a second, before standing. "Because I can't do this anymore. Unless I get over you, there's no way I can have a successful relationship with anyone else."

A trickle of fear spread through me. "Are you saying that we can't be friends anymore?"

"That depends." He reached for my hand and pulled me from the bed. We stood close enough for his every breath to stir my hair. He guided his palm across my cheek. "How do you feel about me?"

"I…I…"

Ding. Dong.

Deke waited for the chimes of the doorbell to stop. "That's Sheila, isn't it?"

I made a small nod. "I guess I have to go."

We stood so close now, I could almost taste his lips.

"I…I have to get out of here," I mumbled as I moved his hand from my face. "I need to think about some things."

He took a step back. "Go have some fun. I'll be here when you get back."

I walked toward the door and stopped to look back at him. "Promise?" I whispered.

"Promise."

CHAPTER 17

"Damn."

I frowned at Sheila. "Is that all you have to say?"

She nodded. "Yep, that pretty much sums it up."

I crossed my arms and turned toward the window before spinning back toward her. "I can't believe what he said! How can he just drop something like that on me?"

"You should have seen it coming a long time ago."

"What?"

"Anybody with half a brain could figure out Deke was in love with you," Sheila said. "I mean, who else but someone who loved you would put up with your craziness for such a long time?"

"You're saying I'm dumb?"

She shrugged. "Sometimes, you can't see the manure cause you're standing in the shit."

"What?"

"Yeah, that never made any sense to me, either. It was something my granddaddy used to say."

I held my head in my hands. "I can't believe he did this to me."

"Well, how do you feel about him?"

I twirled my hair around my finger. "Umm...he's cool."

"Cool?"

"You know what I mean," I said. "He's my best friend. I'm not in love with him or anything."

Sheila stared at me.

"What? You act like you don't believe me?"

She pulled into her driveway. "I don't."

I followed Sheila out of the car and into the house. "Why is it so hard for you to believe I don't love him?"

"Because you do," she said. "You should see the way you look at him. The way you say his name." She laughed. "You remind me of Jack and my mother."

"Who reminds you of Jack and myself?" a voice said from around the corner. I followed Sheila into the kitchen, where Veronica sat on a stool at her breakfast bar.

"I'm trying to convince Maxine that she's in love with Deke."

Veronica didn't look up from the paper. "Stop pressing her, dear. She'll figure it out eventually."

I couldn't believe I was hearing this. "Does everyone in this town think I'm in love with my best friend?"

They looked at each other and nodded. "Yep."

I pulled up a stool and sat beside my soon-to-be stepmother. "If everyone else knows, why don't I?"

"Because you see only what you want to see," Veronica said. "You don't let people get very close to you, do you?"

I turned away from her. "What does that have to do with any-thing?"

"It amazes me how much you and Jack are alike," Veronica said. She looked at Sheila before continuing. "A long time ago, I thought I was in love with a man that didn't treat me so nice. And it took me a long time and a lot of hard years to figure out I didn't love him. I just don't want you to spend unnecessary years looking for something that's right in front of your face." She squeezed my hand before letting it go and going back to her newspaper. "Please believe me when I say I'm not trying to tell you how you should feel, or what you should do. I'm just stating what I see. When you want to see it, you will."

I grabbed a banana from the fruit basket and began peeling it. "Do you have anything to chip in?" I asked Sheila.

She shook her head. "Nope. If you want to be an idiot and—"

"Sheila…," her mother began.

She sighed. "If you want to be…foolish and believe you don't feel for him what he feels for you, that's your business." Sheila shrugged. "Maybe Abby can still win him over."

Sheila ducked as the banana peel I threw at her flew over her head. "Okay, maybe not," she replied. She stood from her barstool. "Let's go shopping. This mushy talk is giving me cramps."

"Where to first?" I asked.

Veronica and Sheila looked at each other again. "The beauty salon," they chimed.

Unbelievable. Utterly, totally, completely unbelievable.

The hairdresser leaned over to Sheila. "Is she okay? She hasn't said anything in five minutes."

I wanted to answer her, but my vocal chords had dropped somewhere between my lungs and my small intestine.

"Well, say something," Sheila said as she pinched my arm. "Do you like it or not?"

I finally pried my gaze away from the mirror. "Wow."

"Is that a good thing or bad thing?" the hairdresser asked.

I smiled. "A good thing. Definitely a good thing."

"So you like it?" Sheila asked.

"Like it? I love it! Feel how soft it is," I said as I grabbed Sheila's hand and planted it on my hair.

She rolled her eyes. "Your hair was always soft."

"And look how straight it is."

"I still think you should have left it like it was. I would have killed for curly hair like yours." Sheila took her wallet out of her purse.

"Wait, I can't let you pay for this."

"You don't have a choice," she said as she handed the hairdresser a few bills. "Anyway, I'm not paying for it. Mom is."

"Nice Mom. Maybe she could pass some pointers on to my mother." I followed Sheila out of the shop. "What's next?"

Sheila waved the wad of money under my nose. "Mom said not to bring you home until we've spent every cent of this money."

I frowned. "What else do I need?"

Sheila took my face and tilted it up. "Ever heard of makeup?"

Before I could answer, Sheila had me at a makeup counter, trying on stuff I had never even heard of before.

And that's how the rest of the afternoon went. Over a four-hour span, Sheila dragged me to all ends of the mall. In addition to the new hairdo, I got a bag full of makeup and a brand new wardrobe. I swear, I had more clothes in those bags than some third-world countries did.

Finally, well after all of my energy was gone, we spent the last of the money on ice cream and headed to the car.

"How do you feel," Sheila asked as we dropped our bags into the trunk.

"Tired."

She smiled. "Shopping can do that to you."

I opened the door and fell into the car. "The only thing I want to do now is go to bed."

She shook her head. "Not yet. We have one more stop to make first."

My eyes widened. "If I have to walk into one more dressing room...."

"No more dressing rooms," she said. "We're going to the bowling alley."

I frowned. "I don't know how to bowl."

"Neither do I."

"Then why are we going?"

Sheila started the car and gave me a sly smile. "You'll see."

I walked into the bowling alley behind Sheila and tried not to choke on the clouds of cigarette smoke that hung in the air. The bowling alley was just as loud as it was smoky. It seemed as if the entire student population of Chickasha had been crammed into the building.

"Doesn't anyone have anything better to do with their evenings?" I asked.

"Tonight is teen night," Sheila said. "High school and college students get half-off for every game." She nodded toward the food area. "Let's get something to eat. I'm starving."

"We just had dinner," I said.

"That was over forty-five minutes ago," Sheila replied as she walked up to the counter. A somewhat cute Hispanic boy was standing behind the register, taking orders. Sheila smirked at him. "Let me get two hot dogs, one with extra relish, the other with extra onions, a large order of fries…and a diet soda."

"Anything else?"

She winked at him. "Yeah, and your phone number."

The guy looked like he wanted to run the other way. I laughed and found a seat.

As Sheila waited on her food, I watched all of the teenage bowlers. In one lane, a guy was teaching a girl how to bowl and probably getting some cheap feels in as well. In another lane, a group of friends sat and laughed together, with one of the girls smiling and sitting in some guy's lap. The way she was draped over him, you would think she did-n't have a backbone.

I shook my head. If there was anything I hated, it was PDA. Public Displays of Affection.

"What are you gawking at?" Sheila asked as she dropped into the chair across from me.

"Nothing of importance." I nodded toward the boy at the register. "Did he give you his phone number?"

She shook her head. "Naw, I let him off the hook." She took a bite of one of her hot dogs. "You think I'm desperate, don't you? Always throwing myself at boys."

"Desperate?" I gasped. "What could possibly make me think something like that?"

Sheila rolled her eyes. "Funny."

I leaned closer to her. "Are you desperate?"

Sheila laughed so hard she snorted soda out of her nose. "For these knuckleheads? Are you crazy?" She wiped her face. "Ouch, that burns."

She stuffed some fries in her mouth. "I may seem crazy to the rest of the world, but as long as I'm comfortable with myself, I'm okay."

I frowned. "It doesn't bother you that you don't fit in?"

"It used to. And I can't lie—sometimes it still does. But I have to be true to myself first. I love the way I am, and if no one else does, screw 'em."

All of a sudden, Sheila looked a lot older than sixteen.

I picked up the metal napkin dispenser on the table and took a good look at myself. My lips were strawberry red, and my cheeks were pink and rosy. I touched the bangs over my forehead. I looked like an entirely different person, felt like an entirely different person. I looked down at my perfectly shaped fingernails and the expensive clothes I had on. I could have easily substituted for any of the other girls in the bowling alley. Same hair, same clothes, same makeup.

"I look just like those girls out there," I said, more to myself than to Sheila.

"Yes, you do. But isn't that what you want? Don't you want to fit in?"

"Yes," I said. I paused and shook my head. "No."

Sheila slurped on her drink and stared at me.

"I mean, it would be nice, but that's not me. I'm not them." I grabbed a napkin, and wiped the lipstick off my lips. "The old me would never get caught wearing this crap."

"Then why are you wearing it now?"

"Because I'm different now. I'm white."

She nodded to the people bowling. "So, you're like them?"

I shuttered. "I hope not."

"Then what are you?"

"I'm...me."

I looked down at my clothes, then back at Sheila. "You sly little bastard," I said as I began to smile. "You did this on purpose, didn't you?"

"It took you long enough. I was getting tired of walking around with you. Ralph Lauren and Tommy Hilfiger should be paying you, with all the advertising you're doing for them."

Sheila reached over and grabbed my hand. "You're white and black, Maxine. Accept it, but don't let it change who you are."

I smiled. "Thanks, Sheila...sister."

Sheila smiled the purest smile I had ever seen. "Sister," she whispered. "I'm gonna have a sister."

"Scary, isn't it."

She nodded. "Now look what you made me do," she said as she dabbed at her eyes with a napkin. "You've got me looking like a little bitch, with all of this crying."

"Believe me, I don't look any better in this get-up," I said. "Are you ready to get out of here?"

"Of course," she said, pushing herself away from the table. "I feel like I'm stuck in a Gap commercial.

"What are you gonna do about Deke?" she asked as we exited the bowling alley.

"I don't know. I haven't figured out how I feel yet."

"No, you just haven't admitted to yourself how you feel. If I were you, I'd...." Sheila stopped walking.

"What?" I asked. But before the words were out of my mouth, I knew why Sheila had stopped. Marcus and a group of boys were walking toward us. A few of them carried bottles in brown paper bags, others puffed on cigarettes.

"Look who we have here?" Marcus said. "Two crazy white bitches. Is this freaks' night, or what?"

I began to tense up, but relaxed once I felt Sheila's hand on my shoulder. "Calm down, Maxine," she said. "It's not worth it."

"Yeah, Maxine, listen to your girl." Marcus reeked of marijuana and cheap alcohol. He looked back at the group of people behind him. "Maybe Sheila doesn't feel so high and mighty without her shotgun. Let me turn back around, before I get a couple of shells in my back like her pop did."

"You're just mad cause I wouldn't have sex with you," I said. "Your drunk ass probably wouldn't have lasted but two minutes anyway."

The group behind him erupted into a chorus of groans. Some of them couldn't even stand up straight, they were laughing so hard. Then again, they could have just been drunk.

"Shut up," he yelled at them. He spun toward me and almost spilled his cup of beer. "Nobody wants your trifling ass anyway," he said. "No one except for that punk ass friend of yours."

I took a step closer to Marcus. "That's right, Deke wants me. He treats me with respect and he talks to me like I'm a person, not a piece of meat." I was directly in Marcus's face by now, poking at his chest. "So your no-game, non-talking, foul-breathed, butt-ugly, wanna-be gansta ass can keep on walking."

Sheila stepped up behind me and flipped something at Marcus. I watched as a peppermint bounced off his chest and fell to the ground.

"Try it sometime," she said between giggles. "It does wonders."

At first, I couldn't tell if Marcus was embarrassed or mad. He sneered at us while putting his hand to his face. He took a quick whiff of his breath and jumped back from his hand. That made his boys laugh even more.

Marcus looked so mad I thought the vein on his forehead was going to burst. "Fuck y'all," he yelled as he threw his cup at us. Before we could move, we were drenched with beer. It was in our hair, in our faces, on our clothes. It was everywhere.

Everyone got quiet. I looked down at myself, looked at Sheila, and looked back at Marcus. He had a sick smile on his face.

I reached down and pulled off one of my heels. "Sheila, hold these please. I'm 'bout to beat his ass."

I started toward him, but Sheila pulled me back. "Come on Maxine, let's just go."

Marcus took a fresh bottle from one of the boys. "I knew that bitch wasn't going to do anything," he said to the group.

Before he could even take a sip of his beer, I had sidestepped Sheila, and was bashing Marcus's face in. Seconds later, Sheila was on his back, clutching at his neck.

"Yeah, who's the bitch now," she yelled as he struggled for air.

I kept punching at him. When most girls fight, they usually swing their arms and yell a lot. Basically, they look like big, loud windmills. But today, I wasn't fighting like a girl. Every blow I made solidly connected with some part of Marcus's body.

I squeezed my eyes shut and jabbed at his midsection. I wanted to punch out all of the bitches, sluts, niggers, and whatever other slurs I could from his body. I was punching so hard, I didn't notice the blue lights flashing around us, until I was being pried away from Marcus.

"Leave me alone," I yelled as I tried to jump back at Marcus. But strong, thick hands held me in place.

"Young lady, be still," someone said. "You're under arrest."

It was then that I looked at the person restraining me. He wore a blue uniform, with a badge, and he didn't look very happy.

I forced a half smile. "Oops."

CHAPTER 18

"How many times do I have to say that I'm sorry?" I asked as Jack and I sped away from the police station. "It wasn't my fault."

He didn't respond.

I sighed. "Where's Sheila? Please don't tell me you left her in there."

Jack looked at me. "Veronica picked her up a few minutes ago."

Finally he was talking. "Jack, I'm sorry—"

"You don't know how disappointed I am in you," Jack said. "You could have killed him."

I rolled my eyes. "It wasn't that serious."

"You never think it's that serious, until things get out of hand. Then you end up paying for an accident for the rest of your life." He spun toward me. "Do you want to be in jail for the rest of your life?"

I meekly shook my head. "No."

"Well, you'd better start acting like it. You can't fight everyone that makes you mad."

I couldn't believe he was taking up for Marcus. I waved my finger at him. "How do you know what I can and can't do? You were never around to teach me right from wrong, *Dad*."

Jack pressed his lips together and faced the road. "This has nothing to do with me not being there before—"

"This has everything to do with it. I'm not a little girl anymore. You can't start being a father now." I shook my head. "Maybe coming out here was a mistake."

He was silent for a second before replying, "Maybe so."

We rode the rest of the trip home in silence, with me on my side of the truck, and him on his side.

Maybe it really was a mistake coming here. Maybe Jack and I were too different to close the rift between us. Then again, maybe we were too alike.

He pulled into the yard but didn't turn off the engine. I sat with my arms crossed, waiting for a new argument.

"What are you doing tomorrow morning?" he asked.

"Packing."

He frowned. "I want to take you somewhere." He looked at his watch. "I have to go to the hospital, but I'll be back home tomorrow morning. Be ready."

I didn't respond to him. I just got out of the truck. He waited until I was inside the house before he backed out and pulled away.

I couldn't believe I got arrested. What on earth was I thinking? Mom was going to have a heart attack when she found out.

I walked by Deke's room. I contemplated knocking on the door, but decided against it. I had enough on my mind; the last thing I wanted to do was confront Deke. I laughed to myself. If he loved me today, he'd love me tomorrow.

Maybe.

I climbed into the truck and slammed the door shut. "Let's get this over with."

Jack started the engine. "Hello to you, too."

We pulled out of the driveway and began our journey, although I had no idea what our end destination was.

"Jack, where the hell are we going?"

"Such language," he muttered. "We're going someplace...sacred."

"I'm not going to anything that has to do with religion. No revivals, no faith healers, no medicine men, nothing!"

Jack laughed. "What injustice did God do to you this morning? Did he put too much milk in your coffee?"

I continued to stare ahead.

The familiar landmarks of Main Street came and went. We drove by the church, but Jack didn't even slow down. The farther we went out, the antsier I became. Where was he taking me?

"I talked to Veronica this morning," Jack said as we cruised down a desolate highway. "I heard all about what happened between you and Marcus." There was an apologetic tone to his voice. "I had no idea Marcus was the way he was."

"See, I told you it wasn't my fault—"

"Hold up," he said. "You have to always be in control of yourself, Maxine. You can't blame your actions on others." He slowed down, and pulled down a dusty trail.

"What was I supposed to do, walk away?"

"Yes."

I pushed my lips out. "Umph, easy for you to say."

He paused. "You're right, it's very easy for me to say."

I frowned and looked at Jack. His eyes stared ahead, but they didn't seem to be focused at all on the road. They were distant, off in another time, another place.

He parked alongside the edge of the road. "Come with me. I want to show you something."

We climbed out of the truck and walked in silence. I had only been out of the air-conditioned truck for a few seconds, but I could already feel trickles of sweat running down my back. After being out in this beating sun, I wouldn't have to worry about my skin tone anymore.

I slowed when I saw the first tombstone. Then another. Suddenly, I was surrounded by a village of them.

"Why are we in a cemetery?"

Jack either ignored my question, or he never heard me to begin with. His eyes had the same glazed over look they had had earlier in the truck. He took a couple more steps, before stopping in front of a tombstone.

I crept around it and looked at the engraving.

Raymond Bozier Stevenson.

I inhaled hard, and felt a sharp pain in my chest. Jack stared at the tombstone, clinching and unclenching his fists.

"It's him, isn't it? The man that you killed."

He didn't respond.

"Why did you bring me here?" I asked. "This isn't funny."

"It wasn't meant to be funny," he finally said. He turned to me. "Maxine, we're both so much alike."

"I'm nothing like you. I don't murder people."

"You're distant," he said. "You don't let people into your life. You don't fit in. You blame everyone else for your problems. You run from your problems instead of facing them."

I wanted to put my hands over my ears. "I—I don't do that."

"Maxine, look at me." He took my hands and held me still. "I'm not trying to scare you. I just don't want you to make the same mistakes I did." He turned my body so I faced the gravesite. "Let me ask you a question: Was it my fault that he ended up dead?"

"Of course—you killed him."

"But I didn't realize what I was doing," he continued. "I didn't mean to do it."

"What you did and what I did last night are two different things."

"Of course they're different. I killed a man. You just put someone in the hospital."

I gasped. "Hospital?"

He nodded. "You broke one of Marcus's ribs. You came extremely close to puncturing his lung."

Jack let go of my hands and I felt myself sinking to the ground. My knees fell against the hard earth. I couldn't believe how badly I had hurt Marcus.

Jack sat down beside me. "You know, I used to believe I was a failure. I was a failure in the ministry, a failure as a father, a failure as a husband—a basic fuck-up."

I looked up at Jack. "You cursed."

He shrugged. "Sue me. Anyway, it wasn't until a lot later that I learned in order to live my life to the fullest, I had to let go of the past. I had to let go of all of the hatred and anger I felt."

"What were you so angry at?"

"Take your pick. My father. Your mother. Raymond. God. Everything in my life. I blamed everyone and everything else for my problems.

"The thing was, it didn't matter who was at fault for my problems. They were my problems and I was the one that had to deal with them."

"How did you start?" I asked.

"By accepting my past mistakes and working to deal with my own problems. That's why I decided to come back here instead of trying to start over somewhere else. I couldn't run anymore."

"That's why you won't leave the church?"

He nodded. "I love that church. It was the only place to accept me with open arms. I'll be the first to admit, sometimes so called Christians can be the most judgmental people around."

"Why don't you preach?" I asked. "You could go back to school, finish your degree—"

He shook his head. "It was never my calling to preach. I wanted to be a musician. But Joseph Phillips wouldn't hear of his only son being anything other than a preacherman. Don't get me wrong, I love the Lord, but He has a different calling for every person." He paused. "Even for you."

I rolled my eyes. "We're actually having a good conversation; don't screw it up."

He held up his hands. "You win, for now."

An ant was steadily making its way up my leg, much like Marcus was the other night. I started to crush it but stopped. Instead, I brushed it off and watched it scurry away in the other direction. "I can't believe I'm sitting here in the middle of a cemetery, on top of dead people."

He stood up and helped me to my feet. "This is the first time I've been out here since before I was incarcerated. I'm almost surprised I remembered where the gravesite was."

"Almost?"

He ran his fingers along the edge of the tombstone. "There are some things you never forget."

We stood in front of the tombstone a few minutes, not saying anything. A few renegade tears streaked down Jack's face. He didn't bother to wipe them away. A part of me was shocked to see him crying. I had never seen a man cry before.

We started back toward the truck. The sun was in our faces now. I walked behind Jack and tried to take refuge in his shadow. Suddenly, he stopped walking. "Maxine, stay behind me. And whatever happens, don't be scared."

"How am I not supposed to feel scared when everything you do tells me to be scared?" I shielded my eyes from the sun and peeked around him. A lone figure, maybe a man, walked toward us.

"The groundskeeper said he thought he saw you," the man said. "What the hell are you doing here?"

Jack kept one hand on me, while trying to block the intense sunlight from his face with his other hand. "We didn't mean any trouble."

"That's what you said over twenty years ago when you killed my boy, you son of a bitch."

My mouth gaped open. It was Raymond's father.

Jack took slow steps toward the man. The man was like a guard, standing between us and the freedom of the truck. All he needed was a weapon.

As if he read my mind, he reached into the burlap sack slung over his shoulder and pulled out a shotgun.

Me and my overactive imagination.

"Mr. Stevenson, I'm sorry for coming here. My daughter and I are on our way out."

"Daughter?" He walked closer to us. "So, this is your famous nigger daughter."

I was too busy being scared to flinch at his harsh words. I could clearly see him now. He wore brown, faded corduroy pants and a plaid shirt that had long ago seen its glory years. The stubble on his face was a salt and pepper mix. His front tooth was chipped and his chin jutted out like a beak on a bird.

"You know how unfair it is for me to be robbed of a child while you're blessed with one?" He waved the shotgun at us. "What's that they say about an eye for an eye?"

Jack's body snapped taunt. "Mr. Stevenson, if you lay one hand on her, so help me God I'll—"

"You'll what? Kill me like you did Raymond?" He peered at me, with a wicked scowl on his face. "It's funny; with the hair, she don't look much black. She's almost normal." He came closer. "She looks a lot like your momma."

I brought my hand to my head and fingered my straightened reddish locks. I had almost forgotten about the new hairdo I had gotten at the salon yesterday.

He spit out a wad of tobacco dangerously close to my feet. "When's the last time you spoke to your daddy?"

I could hear Jack's teeth grinding together. "Why are you bringing him up?"

"He ain't doing so good. The doctor say he got three, maybe four months left."

I frowned. The way he was talking, it sounded like Jack's father was still alive.

Mr. Stevenson eyed us one more time as if he was trying to decide what to do with us. Jack grabbed a tight hold of my hand.

"This was your last warning, Phillips," he said. "If I see you out here ever again…." He finished his statement by lowering his gun and stepping out of the way. Jack nodded and we began toward the truck.

"I'll tell Joe I saw you," he yelled. "I'm sure he'll be tickled to hear that."

Jack didn't turn around. He kept plowing toward the truck, dragging me behind him. We got in the truck and he sped off.

A RED POLKA DOT IN A WORLD FULL OF PLAID

He finally slowed down when he reached the main highway. I started to speak, but didn't. There was no need to ask a question to which I already knew the answer.

My grandfather was alive.

CHAPTER 19

Jack pulled into the driveway. We sat in the truck, in silence, as we had the entire trip back home. I didn't know what to say; maybe he didn't either.

Finally I turned to him. "You lied to me."

"I didn't lie, Maxine. My father *is* dead, to a certain degree."

"You're about four months too early. Maybe we should have this conversation then."

He sighed. "He disowned me. The last time I saw my father, he told me to treat him as if he were dead." He shrugged. "I was never one to argue with the man."

"I can't believe you weren't going to tell me that my grandfather is still alive," I said. "You're just as bad as Mom."

"Believe me, he's not any grandfather you would want."

"How do you know?" I snapped. "You've never given me the opportunity to make that choice. In a few months, there won't be much of a choice to make."

"Just let the old man die."

"Weren't you just saying something about letting go of your anger?" I asked. "It seems like you haven't followed your own advice."

Jack's face was contorted into a half frown, half sneer. "When I needed him the most, he abandoned me. He drove me away from the only home, the only family I had." Jack's eyes were wide and full of emotion. "I have survived without one stray word from that man for over twenty years. Why should I waste my time even thinking about him now?"

"Because I'm your daughter, and I'm asking you."

He frowned and stared at the steering wheel. "What do you want to do, meet him?"

"That's exactly what I want to do."

"Maxine—"

"For all of my life, I've been alone. Now I'm finding out that I have this family, this side of me that I never knew existed. I have to see him, if only once." I paused. "I took a big risk when I came out here to figure out who you were," I said. "At least give me the opportunity to learn who he is, too."

"What if he doesn't want to see you?" he asked.

"Then I can go back home knowing I tried."

Jack shook his head. "Please don't do this."

"I have to."

He sighed and dropped his head. "Tomorrow afternoon. I get off work at noon and I'll be home around two."

I nodded and climbed out of the truck. Jack didn't follow. "Aren't you coming in?"

He shook his head. "I need to drive around, clear my thoughts. I'll probably spend the night at Veronica's."

I flashed him a dirty look. "I didn't think deacons were supposed to—"

"Don't start." He cranked up the truck. "See you tomorrow."

I waved and watched him drive off down the street. It wasn't late at all, but I was extremely tired. I had only gotten a few hours of sleep last night, and today's events had taken their toll on my body.

Was Jack right about his father? Was he really someone I didn't want to meet? As much as his warning shook me, I was determined to piece a family together. I had found a father; a grandfather was the next logical step.

I had never known my mother's parents. They died before I was born—I had seen their gravesites, so I felt pretty confident about that. Mom was an only child, so I didn't have any aunts or uncles or cousins. It had always been me and her, on our own. The idea of having a bigger, fuller, complete family was just too tempting for me to ignore.

I walked straight to my room and collapsed on the bed. I didn't see Deke's car outside, which was just as well. I still didn't know what to say to him. What do you say to a guy when he tells you that he loves you?

I woke up a few hours later. The sun had set, and the crickets had already started their evening operas. I walked to the bathroom and peeled my clothes off. It felt like I was pulling dried candle wax from my body. If I never saw another sunny day again, I wouldn't be sad. In the shower, I took extra time to scrub my face. I could still feel the make-up from the day before. Now I knew how clowns felt.

I stepped out of the shower and rummaged through the bathroom cabinets for nail polish remover. I was so tired yesterday I didn't even look for any. After a few moments, I gave up my search. It was just as well—I would have really been worried about Jack had I actually found some.

I crawled into bed and tried to forget everything that had happened to me in the past few days. But every time I closed my eyes, my mind filled with thoughts of Deke, Jack, Deke, my grandfather, Marcus, Deke, and myself.

And did I mention Deke?

I beat up my pillow and tried to find a cool spot in the bed.

Why was it so hard for me to accept that Deke loved me? Was I that much of a loner? I couldn't believe I'd been so wrapped up in myself for so long, I never realized it. Maybe I didn't want to realize it.

Maybe I loved him, too.

I bolted up in bed. What was I thinking? I couldn't be in love with Deke. He wasn't the type of guy I could fall in love with.

And Marcus was?

I chewed on the inside of my cheek. Maybe it wouldn't be so bad loving him.

I wanted to scream. Things couldn't be this complicated. Either I loved him or I didn't. Simple as that.

I pushed back my sheets and crept out of my room. I took slow, timid steps down the hallway, until I was at Deke's door.

I stood there for a few moments, trying to wipe the sweat from my palms. My body was energized, like all of my muscles were on a caffeine high. I had brushed my teeth moments before, but now my mouth felt like it was stuffed with oatmeal. I took a deep breath and opened the door.

It took a second for my eyes to adjust to the dark. I took a couple of steps toward the bed.

The way Deke slept, it looked like both of his arms were broken. His sheets lay half off the bed, half wrapped around his legs—his strong, thick, chocolate covered legs. My gaze drifted from his legs, to his thighs, to his—

I slapped myself. This was ridiculous. I shouldn't be looking at Deke like that; he was my best friend. I looked back at him.

He must have been eating his Wheaties.

I picked up the sheet from the floor and attempted to cover him back up. I brought it up, but stopped when I noticed the three long scratches I had etched into his arm.

I ran my fingers over the scratches and muffled the soft whimper that crept from my throat. That fool. I told him to let me put some alcohol on it. I slowly placed my lips to his arm and lightly brushed each scratch with a kiss.

Before I knew it, I had climbed on top of him and pulled the sheet over us.

He stirred and his eyes fluttered open.

"What the—Maxine?" he muttered as he rubbed his eyes. "What are you doing?"

"Why me?"

"Huh?"

I propped myself up on my elbows. "Why did you have to go and fall in love with me? I'm sure there are more worthy girls out there."

Deke sighed and looked at me. More like, he looked into me. Him and those eyes. Sometimes I felt naked under his gaze. But that didn't bother me at all. It was so comfortable, so natural. Like it was the way it was supposed to be.

"Maxine, I didn't choose to love you. It just happened."

"Things don't just happen."

He shrugged. "Maybe it was divine intervention."

I frowned. "Cute," I said as I placed my head on his bare chest. I listened to the steady beat of his heart while I searched for the right words.

"I'm scared," I finally said.

I felt his strong fingers rub and caress my back. "I am, too."

"What happens if one day you wake up and don't love me anymore? What happens to our friendship?"

"We're Deke and Maxine," he said. "Our friendship is strong enough to take anything. Don't you agree?"

I nodded.

"Anyway, I don't think I could stop loving you if I wanted to. Believe me, I've tried."

I looked up and slapped him on the arm. "I'm trying to be serious."

"I am, too. As long as you want me, I'll never leave you."

I slid up so that we were almost face to face. His breath came slow and steady across my face. "Promise?" I whispered.

He nodded. "Promise." He ran his fingers through my hair. "Did you do something to your hair? It looks a little different."

That's right, I hadn't seen Deke in the past couple of days. It was amazing how two people could live under the same roof and avoid each other.

"You wouldn't believe my past few days," I said. "I found out I had a grandfather, got arrested, and—"

"Grandfather? Arrested? What? How?"

I shook my head and pressed my finger against his lips. "Don't worry, everything is under control. Jack was a little upset, but it's cool. Marcus isn't in the hospital anymore."

"Marcus? Hospital? Maxine, what did you do?"

"You wouldn't believe me if I told you."

He smiled. "I always believe you."

"You do?"

"When you're sincere, I do." He tightened his embrace. "Do you want to talk about it?"

"No, not tonight."

We were silent for a few moments, staring at each other, just being Deke and Maxine.

"Maxine," he said, with a deep rumble in his voice. "Why are you here? What do you want from me?"

I closed my eyes. The words that had been in my heart for so long were bubbling to the surface, and there wasn't anything I could do about it. There wasn't anything I wanted to do about it.

"Deke, what happens tomorrow? And the day after that?"

"That depends on tonight."

"I love you."

"I know."

My eyes flashed open. There was a large grin on his face. I slapped him again on the arm. "Don't tell me everyone knew except me."

"If it makes you feel better, I was one of the last people to start believing it."

"I don't know whether to choke you or kiss you."

He pulled me closer to him and smiled with his eyes. "I'm not giving you an option."

Suddenly, I was wrapped in the softest, sweetest, warmest kiss I had ever experienced. His lips fell into rhythm with mine. His tongue danced circles around mine.

I pressed myself closer to him. His hands swept through my hair and down my back. I arched with every trace of his fingertips against my skin. My body ached with every fervent, burning kiss.

We slowly pulled apart. "Did you know it would be like that?" I asked.

Deke seemed to be struggling to catch his breath. "I never would have guessed."

We stared at each other for a second before resuming our kisses. Slow kisses and fast kisses, light kisses and heavy kisses. Tender, delicate, loving kisses.

"Wait," I finally said as I forced myself to pull away from his embrace. "What are we doing?"

"I don't know."

"Do you want to stop?"

He paused for a second. "No. Do you?"

Instead of answering his question, I rose from the bed. I ran to my room, grabbed my purse, and searched through it until I found what I was looking for.

Deke was just walking out of his room when I returned. He had a concerned look on his face.

"Maxine, I'm sorry if—"

I smothered his words with a kiss and pushed him back into the room. I closed the door and made sure it was locked. I handed him the condoms.

He looked down at his hand and looked back at me. "Maxine, are you sure about this?"

I stepped to him and pulled his face to mine. Our lips melted into each other's. My hands floated down his back, then across his chiseled chest, as he gently explored my body.

He took my hand and led me to the bed. He sat down, and drew me on top of him. He slowly began to undress me, all the while kissing my entire body. A moan slipped from my lips. I pressed against him, felt all of him. We kissed and caressed, and slid underneath the covers.

I awoke to a flurry of kisses across my face. I slowly opened my eyes to see Deke's face illuminated by the sunlight from the window.

"Good morning," he whispered as he placed another kiss on my nose.

I smiled and drew his face to mine, so I could taste his lips again. "Good morning to you, too. What time is it?"

"Almost eight."

I snuggled against him. It was then that I realized I was hugging up against a very naked body with a very naked body.

"Did we…"

"Yep," he replied.

"How many times…"

"Twice."

"Oh." My thoughts drifted back to last night and I could feel my face getting hot. "I remember."

Deke traced a finger up and down my arm. "While we're talking about last night…sorry about that little accident the first time." He chuckled. "I guess I was a little nervous and—"

"Don't worry about it," I said. "Believe me, the second time more than made up for it."

"Really?"

I ran my fingers down Deke's back and felt a slight tremor run down my own spine. "Oh, yeah." I kissed his chest, once in the center and once on each peck. "Where did you learn to do all of that?"

"Me?" Deke was dark, but I could still see the tiniest hints of a blush. "What about you? You were spectacular. But, you always are."

It was my turn to blush.

"So now what?" I asked. "You know we can't go back to how things were before."

"Was that ever an option?"

"No, I guess not." I shuttered a little.

"Cold?"

I nodded.

Deke pulled me closer to him and our legs intertwined. His body, his skin was warm. I felt myself disappearing into his arms.

"When is Jack getting back?" he asked as he brushed a stray strand of hair from my face.

"Sometime this afternoon." I sighed. "I guess we can't stay like this forever."

"You know, I never tell you how beautiful you are."

I scowled at him. "Deke, are you getting mushy on me?"

He pressed himself against me. "Does this seem mushy?"

I rolled my eyes. "We really have to get up."

By now, he was kissing me along my neck.

I smiled and pulled the covers around us. "Well, it would be a shame to let all of those condoms go to waste...."

"Stop looking at me like that," I said as Deke and I cleaned up the kitchen.

We had just eaten our first meal as a couple. Deke had tried to surprise me with breakfast in bed. Soupy grits and burnt toast had never tasted so good.

"This is how I always looked at you." He slightly bumped me with his hip. "You were just too busy drooling over Marcus to notice."

I submerged my hands back in the hot, soapy water. "You're probably right." I washed a glass and handed it to him. "Should we tell Jack?"

Deke almost dropped the glass. "No! Are you crazy? He'll—"

"Deke, calm down. I'm not talking about...*that*. I was talking about whether we should tell Jack that we're together."

His face relaxed. "I thought you meant tell him about last night."

"I'm bold, but I'm not crazy." I pictured Jack throwing Deke across the room. "No, I think last night will be our little secret for a while."

"A long while," he said. Deke turned off the water and walked away from the sink. He sat at the table and stared blankly at the wall.

The air in the room suddenly seemed to turn chilly. "What's wrong? You don't regret what happened last night, do you?"

He flashed me a smile. "Regret? I have no regrets about last night. Or this morning, for that matter." We shared a secret, reminiscing laugh between ourselves. "If anything, I regret not telling you sooner."

I wiped my hands on a dishtowel and walked to the table. "Then what's wrong? And don't lie and say that it's nothing; I know you better than that."

He placed his hand on mine. "We sinned last night."

I rolled my eyes. "Not this crap."

"Maxine, you know how important my religion is to me. Whether you believe it or not, I know that we—*I*—sinned last night. I was weakened by the temptations of the flesh."

I yanked my hand from under his and walked back to the sink. "You make what we did last night sound like an orgy or something."

"I'm sorry," he said as he rose from the table. He walked behind me and wrapped his arms around my waist. "What we did was magical, beautiful—"

"Don't forget spectacular."

He laughed. "Spectacular. But it was still a sin. And I have to face the repercussions of my actions."

I spun around and looked at him. "You think God's gonna strike you down just because you had sex—or rather, made love—to me last night."

"And this morning," he chirped in.

I didn't bother to laugh. "What type of God would punish you for sharing something so wonderful with the person you love?" I paused. "Did I just say that? I've been watching the Lifetime Channel way too much. Remind me to wash my mouth out with soap."

"Fornication is a sin."

"Because some book says so?"

"Because that's what I believe," he said. "Why is it so hard for you to respect my religion?"

"Your religion makes no sense."

"Sometimes, it's the only thing in the world that makes sense."

I pushed his hands off me. "You're so closed minded. What happens to us if I never embrace your sacred religion? What does God say about that? That we can't be together?"

There was a cold silence in the room. As I stared at Deke, goose bumps popped up along my arms and back. I could feel my bottom lip trembling. *Come on Maxine, the last thing you needed to do was to start crying.*

His eyes seemed to be pleading with me, begging to me. "What do you want me to say, Maxine?" He guided his palm across my cheek. "How else can it be?"

I shook my head. "I'm sure you have better things to do than be with a heretic like me. Shouldn't you be praying or something?"

"Maxine—"

"Just go," I said. I turned away from his powerful gaze. "Leave me alone."

He leaned closer to kiss my cheek, but I pulled back and side stepped him.

He sighed and left the room. And I was alone, once again.

CHAPTER 20

I stared out the window of the truck as Jack parked in front of a large house. The paint was peeling off of the shutters and the walls looked like they badly needed a good scrubbing.

"Are you sure you want to do this?" Jack asked. "It's not too late to turn around."

I shook my head. "I need to do this." I smiled at him. "*We* need to do this."

We exited the truck and began the slow trek across the lawn to the house. The grass was tall but even. It swayed slightly as a cool breeze whisked by us.

Tall maple trees stretched over the house and cast an eerie shadow on the porch. As we ascended the steps to the porch, a wind chime played a not so playful tune.

Jack eyed me once more before knocking on the door. Three hard, distinct raps, like the beginning of a drum cadence.

After a few moments, we heard movement inside the house. The door creaked opened and a woman stuck her head out. "Who is—"

She stopped once her gaze fell upon Jack. She looked as if she was contemplating closing the door. Finally, she opened it completely and stepped onto the porch.

"Hello, Jack," she said as she brushed back her graying hair. A few streaks of red were still left.

"Hello, Aunt Emma," he replied. "I guess you weren't expecting me."

She swiftly nodded, as if that would make the awkwardness pass more quickly.

Jack stepped to the side, so that I was in full view of her. "This is my daughter, Maxine."

A few sparks of life jumped into her eyes. "This is Maxine?" She took a step forward and reached out to me. She seemed to hesitate before placing her wrinkled hand on my head. She brushed my hair, as she had just done hers.

"She's beautiful," she said to Jack. "I never expected her to look like this."

I tried not to feel uncomfortable by her statement, but she must have noticed the slight scowl on Jack's face.

Suddenly her eyes flashed open. "Oh, Jack, I didn't mean…"

"I know you didn't," he said. "Old habits die hard around here." He turned toward me. "This is your Great Aunt Emma. She's your grandmother's sister."

Aunt Emma continued to stoke my hair. "I used to have hair just like yours," she said. "But that was over thirty years ago." She smiled at Jack. "I'm glad you named her after your mother. I feel better knowing there is another Maxine Phillips in the world."

"Mom would have loved her." Jack paused, and his gaze drifted from me to the house. The smile on his face faded away.

"Is he here?" he asked.

She removed her hand from my head and began smoothening her apron. "You know he doesn't want to see you."

"I figured as much," he said. "How is he doing?"

"Not good." Emma's voice was barely a whisper. "Some days, he barely has the energy to stand."

Jack placed his hand on my shoulder. "Tell him we're here."

She nodded, and opened the door. "Do you want to come in?"

"We'd better not," Jack said. "He wouldn't like that."

She nodded again. "It was good seeing you," she said to him. "Even though you were Maxine's child, I always thought of you as the son I never had, especially after she died." She placed her palm on his cheek. "You've always been in my prayers."

She placed a small, motherly kiss on his face before stepping back. The creases around her eyes seemed to intensify as she turned and disappeared into the house.

Jack and I took a few steps back as well, and waited for my grandfather to appear. I had to stuff my hands in my pockets to stop them from shaking. I looked at Jack. His hands were in his pockets, too.

The door creaked open, revealing a frail, withered man. The last remnants of his hair were wispy clouds on his head. His skin seemed to hang loosely to his shriveled body. His eyes were a cold gray that spoke louder than any words could speak.

They said that we were not wanted.

"You've got a lot of nerve, coming here," he finally said. He stood propped up by a walker. His voice was scratchy and faint. "I told you years ago that you weren't welcome here. Did you think I would change my mind?" He pushed himself up on his walker and pointed a crooked, knotty finger at us. "Just as God cast Adam and Eve from the Garden of Eden for their wickedness, so did I to you. Leave, now."

Jack stood firm, neither flinching nor turning away. "I didn't come here for me, Daddy. I came so my daughter could see what was left of her grandfather."

The old man glared at me like a judge passing sentence on a criminal. "The half-breed."

"Her name is Maxine."

"You named her after your mother?" He sneered at me as if he were disgusted with the idea of a black person having the same name as his deceased white wife. He waved his hand in my direction. "I don't care what her name is. My request is still the same. Leave."

I stepped closer to the door and stared into my grandfather's eyes. They were the same gray as mine and Jack's, but they didn't possess any of the spark, any of the fire that ours had.

"My name is Maxine Edrice Phillips and Jack is my father. He's made mistakes, but he's repented for them." I quickly looked at Jack before turning back to the old man at the door. "He's a good man."

My grandfather frowned. "The way I was brought up, children were taught to respect their elders."

I scoffed. "I don't respect anything about you. If Jack isn't your son, then I'm not your granddaughter." I walked back to Jack. "I'm ready to leave."

He smiled at me before looking back at the shell of a man that had once been his father. "Goodbye, Daddy. I wish you more peace in death than you have ever experienced in life."

The walk across the lawn was slow and solemn. Jack continued forward, not looking back even once. We climbed into the truck and pulled onto the road. I glanced briefly at the house. Joseph Phillips had receded to the protection of his small, unforgiving, loveless world.

I turned on the radio, to try to hide the emptiness I felt. "I guess we won't be going to any family reunions anytime soon."

"I got the same feeling," he said. "I'm sorry you had to hear some of the things he said."

"It's okay." I thought back to our conversation in the rose garden. "People can really be ignorant sometimes. They don't understand that love has no color boundary."

I reached over and squeezed his hand. I was almost surprised that I did it. It was too daughter-like.

"Are you okay?" I asked.

"Yeah," he replied. "I don't think I was really able to forgive him until now."

"He doesn't deserve your forgiveness."

Jack shook his head. "My forgiveness isn't for his salvation—it's for mine."

"Salvation," I said, more to myself than to Jack. "Do you think he's going to Hell?"

"You believe in Hell?"

"Yeah, they call it New Jersey."

Jack laughed. "I don't know if he's going to Hell or not. That's between him and God. I'll be praying for him, though."

"What exactly do you do when you pray?"

"Nothing magical," he said. "I thank God for what He's done for me, and my family and friends, and then I ask Him to continue blessing us." Jack looked at me out of the corner of his eye. "Any reason for all of the God questions?"

I scrunched up my nose. "Don't worry, I'm not going to start walking on water or anything like that. It's just…Deke said something to me once. He said that God gives us what we need when we need it, not when we want it. Is that true?"

"That's what I believe," Jack said. "I don't think I would have ever faced my father again if it weren't for you. God knew I needed to do it, but He knew I wasn't ready yet. He knew I needed you."

I sighed. "This is so confusing. Next, you'll tell me that I wasn't ready to be reunited with you until now, and that all of this was part of God's plan."

Jack shrugged. "Well, would you have been able to handle it if, five years ago, I showed up on your doorstep and told you everything about me?"

I continued to stare ahead. I didn't respond to his question, because I didn't want to admit that he was right.

"Maxine, I'm not trying to force you into believing what I believe. I'm just trying to give you another way to look at life." He patted my knee. "Do you have any more questions?"

"No—well, maybe." I cleared my throat and fidgeted with my hands. "Is it true that Christians and non-Christians don't mix?"

Jack turned off the radio. "This is about Deke, isn't it?"

"Yeah," I whispered.

"You love him?"

I nodded.

"He loves you?"

I nodded again.

"The Lord has seriously blessed you, you know."

"Maybe. If God exists."

"He exists," Jack said. "He lives above us, below us, around us, inside of us."

"So do bacteria."

Jack sighed. "I have to pick up some paperwork at the church. It should only take a few minutes."

By the time we got to the church, it was late in the afternoon. I wasn't a big fan of churches, but anything to keep me away from home and Deke made me happy.

"Is that Deke's car?" Jack asked.

I shielded my eyes from the setting sun and squinted out the window. Sure enough, Deke's car sat in the parking lot.

Great. Thanks God.

Jack parked and opened his door. "Are you getting out?"

"I don't think so."

"You mean to tell me that you can take being ridiculed by a bitter old man you've never met before, but you can't go in there and talk to your best friend?"

"Um, yeah, that's exactly what I'm saying."

Jack closed his door back and settled in his seat. "What are you so afraid of?"

I shrugged. "I finally get with a guy I really like, and now I find out we can't be together."

"Because Deke believes in the Lord and you don't?"

I nodded. "Isn't that petty of Deke to—"

"Petty? Maxine, do you realize what you're asking this boy to do? You're asking him to forsake everything he has ever believed in, for you. Deke would be damning himself if he did that."

"He wouldn't be damning himself."

"How do you know?" Jack snapped. "You have to respect Deke's beliefs. His religion is as much a part of him as his name."

"Then what am I supposed to do?" I asked.

"Pray."

I rolled my eyes. "Next you'll be telling me to part the Red Sea."

Jack ignored me. "Praying is just like talking to God."

"Isn't that long distance?"

"Do you love Deke?" he asked.

I nodded. "Very much."

"Then try. It won't hurt anything to try to open up to God. You may be surprised what you find out." He reopened his door and stepped out. "I'm going ahead inside. If you're not in the truck when I get back, I'll assume you're riding with Deke."

I watched him disappear into the church, before getting out of the truck and following him in.

I walked slowly down the hallway, straining to hear any sound. You'd think I would feel safe in the house of God, but churches could be really creepy when no one was there.

I entered the Sanctuary. It looked empty, save for Jesus Christ staring back at me from a stained glass window. He stood with His arms outstretched, and a soft halo circled His head. The last remnants of light floated through the window and cast an almost orange haze in the church.

As I turned to leave, a movement caught my eye. I saw the outline of a figure kneeling in the shadows.

"Deke, is that you?"

The figure stood up and momentarily stepped into the light. Deke stared at me before retreating back to his shaded corner.

I took a deep breath and shuffled forward. I kept my eyes on my shoes the entire time. They were scuffed and scarred. The once glistening white leather had been replaced by a dull, gray griminess. The shoes made a stark contrast to the clean, plush, red carpeting.

I walked up to the front of the church, but stayed in the orange glow of the window. Jesus's eyes had seemed to follow me from the back of the church to the front.

Deke continued to kneel at the pew. The filtered light from the window strained to touch him in the shadows, but he was just out of reach.

"What are you doing?" I asked.

"Praying."

"Oh, I didn't mean to disturb you. I'll leave and—"

"No," Deke said as he rose from his knees. "I was just finishing up."

"How long have you been here?"

"About two hours."

"Two hours?"

"God and I had a lot of things to talk about." He finally stepped out of the shadows. "How was your visit with your grandfather?"

I kept my eyes steady and calm. "I don't have a grandfather."

Deke just nodded, and silence followed. Silence had always been our security blanket, warming us from the cold chill of the truth.

He pounded his fist into his palm. "This is killing me. Do you know how hard this is, trying to choose between you and my God? I've been trying to figure out something—anything—to let me be with you. But...." He let his words dissipate into the orange haze.

"I'll try."

"What?"

I stepped toward him. "I love you, Deke. Too much not to at least try to embrace your God again."

Deke smiled. "He's your God, too."

"That's what people keep on telling me."

His face became serious. "Maxine, you can't do this just because of me. It has to be because you want to."

"I know. Maybe God finally got to me on His list." I glanced at the window. "I can't deny all of the good things that have happened to me. Maybe it was all coincidence or maybe it was divine intervention. I don't know, but I have to find out."

I looked back at Deke. "But I'm gonna need some help getting that praying thing down; it's been a long time since I last did it." He began walking toward me. "And don't get any bright ideas. I'm not getting baptized anytime soon, and I damn sure ain't joining nobody's choir."

Deke scooped me up in his thick, sturdy arms. "I love you so much."

"Yeah, and Happy Hanukkah to you too."

We giggled and stared into each other eyes. The orange glow of the sun surrounded us, and enveloped our embrace.

I cupped my hands around his neck. "I really want to kiss you right now, but…." I nodded toward the stained-glass window of Jesus. "I don't know if I should with Him watching."

Deke laughed and pulled me even closer. "I think He'll make an exception." Deke joined his lips to mine, and the way we kissed, it had to be love. Then he grabbed my hand and pulled me out of the church. Between the door and the car, he managed to plant twenty-some kisses on my lips, neck, cheeks and forehead.

"Isn't this lust?" I said, trying to dry my face on my sleeve. "I know the Bible says something about that."

Deke smiled. "You riding with me?"

I looked around the parking lot. Sure enough, Jack's truck was gone. It was almost as if he knew things would work out between me and Deke.

I climbed into the car. "We're Deke and Maxine; of course I'm riding." I slid my hand over and intertwined my fingers with his. The feel of his skin against mine still sent warm flashes through my body.

Yep, we were definitely going to have a problem with the lust issue.

"Now don't be surprised if this doesn't work out," I said as Deke sped down the highway. "I'll try, but—"

"This is going to work," Deke said. "I have faith in you. And God."

"Yeah, that's what they said about the Titanic." I eyed the speed gage. "Deke, be careful. People love to fly around this corner."

Just then, a pair of headlights appeared. Whatever they belonged to, it was in the wrong lane and charging straight toward us.

"Deke, watch out!"

Deke yanked at the steering wheel and slammed on the brakes. The car skidded and began to spin out of control. Deke threw his arm across me and pushed me back against the seat.

I squeezed my eyes shut, and my world was thrust into darkness.

CHAPTER 21

It was a warm and sunny day in Columbia when we buried Deke. The ceremony was beautiful, just as he would have liked it. Not too long, not too sad. With all the people that attended the funeral, it was apparent that Deke had touched many people's lives, not just my own.

I stood between Mom and Jack, and watched as the black, rich soil slipped between my fingers onto the sleek casket. My other arm hung loosely in a sling, a reminder of the crash I was fortunate enough to survive. I dropped the last of my soil onto the casket, and the men began covering the grave.

"When are y'all leaving to go back?" Mom asked.

"Early tomorrow morning," Jack replied. "Veronica has to be back at work on Monday."

"Oh," Mom said, softly. She looked back at Veronica and Sheila as they talked to Deke's parents. "Well, you have a good trip," she said as she hugged Jack. As my parents embraced each other, I could almost picture them being in love so many years ago.

She shuffled backward a few steps and smoothened his suit. "You take care of yourself, and if you're ever in the area…." She fingered at his lapel and they both shared a fleeting laugh. I turned away and pretended to ignore them.

"This is never easy, is it?" she said.

"It wasn't then, and it isn't now."

She sighed. "Good-bye Jack."

"Good-bye, Katherine."

"Kathy," she said. "Call me Kathy."

I let them continue their farewells in private and walked over to Veronica and Sheila. Veronica's face was stained with dried tears, while Sheila's eyes didn't have a shade of redness to them.

"Jack says that y'all are leaving pretty early tomorrow morning," I said.

Veronica nodded as she reached over and hugged me. "You be good, Maxine," she said, before walking off.

Sheila chuckled. "You couldn't be good if you wanted to." She hugged me also. "Deke was alright." Her voice got soft and she almost seemed vulnerable. "I hate to see a good man brought down in his prime."

Just hearing someone else talk about him, I could feel the tears welling up in my eyes again. I had promised myself I wouldn't cry anymore; you'd think that after a week I'd be out of tears.

"Oh, I'm sorry." Sheila pulled some tissue out of her pocket. "Are you okay?"

I repositioned my sling around my shoulder. "I'll be glad when I get this thing off."

"Yeah, I've worn one or two of those things before. They aren't fun."

We walked a few feet before stopping. "Being that we're practically family, I have a question for you." I bit my lip and hesitated, before opening my mouth. "Did you kill your father?"

Sheila looked at me for a long time, before smiling. "Does it really matter?"

I thought for a moment, then shook my head.

"I think sometimes, you shouldn't ask a question when you don't want to know its answer. Don't you agree?"

I nodded and hugged her again. "Bye, Sheila. See you in a few months."

Most people were heading back to the church by now. The funeral home director was ushering Mr. and Mrs. Ashland toward one of the limousines. One of the drivers came toward me, but I waved him off.

"I think I'll stick around here a little longer," I said.

He nodded, and walked back toward his limousine.

"You're not going to the dinner?"

I turned around. I was almost scared Jack had left without saying good-bye.

"No, I don't feel like being social right now. I'll walk over to the church in a few minutes."

"I understand," he said. We watched as the limousines crossed the street and pulled into the church parking lot.

"I didn't tell you; the guy is going to plead guilty to vehicular homicide."

I shrugged. "Somehow, that doesn't make me feel a lot better. Deke's still gone."

"Are you mad? Bitter?"

"You know, that's what amazes me the most," I said. "I should be furious at Deke, or God, or both of them. But I'm not." I looked back at Deke's fresh grave. "Don't misunderstand, I wish he was still here, but even one moment with him was better than a lifetime of being without him."

"Deke was a very good man," Jack said, more to himself than to me. "I would have liked to call him my son."

The corners of my lips twitched. "He...he was the best."

We walked a few steps, in no particular direction. "I thought you may want to know, I prayed last night," I said.

Jack raised an eyebrow at me.

"Well it was more like I talked, and God listened."

"You believe in God now?"

"I don't know what I believe," I said. "But I do know Deke was sent by someone to watch over me, and help me through a very diffi-cult time of my life."

He beamed. "You don't know how happy I am to hear that. Keep on talking to God and listen for Him to talk back. He won't let you down." Jack leaned over and embraced me. "And neither will I."

We held on to each other for a few minutes. I was afraid to let go, and I think he was, too.

"Good-bye, Maxine," he finally said.

"Bye, Jack. Or should I start calling you Dad?"

Jack pulled away from me, with a startled grin on his face. He shook his head. "No, that would make me feel too old." He stroked my hair. "Seriously, I don't care what you call me, as long as you call me." He began toward the church. "And if you didn't notice, Aunt Emma sent an arrangement."

It was my turn to be shocked. "How did she find out?"

"I don't know. But don't be surprised if we take a few more trips out to the country during Christmas."

I waved and watched my dad, Jack Phillips, disappear into the sunset.

I walked back to Deke's gravesite. The cemetery was empty now. I was alone, but I wasn't lonely.

"I really miss you, Deke," I said as the wind picked up around me. "I know you're somewhere, watching over me, making sure I don't get into too much trouble."

As I knelt at the gravesite, my knees pushed deep into the soft ground. My dress had smudges of dirt on it, but I knew Deke wouldn't mind. "If I make any mistakes, tell God that I'm sorry, but I'm really trying."

I bowed my head. "Our Father, which art in heaven—no scratch that. Uh, dear Lord, thank you for…no, scratch that too." I looked up at the sky. "This is harder than I thought." I sighed and closed my eyes again. "Dear God, thank you for the flowers and the grass and stuff like that. Take care of Deke, I love him very much. Take care of my family and Deke's family, too. And take care of yourself while you're at it. I bet it's a pain being God and having to deal with a cold or a rash or something like that. Anyway, that's it for now. Uh, Amen."

I opened my eyes, smiled at the clouds, and winked. "At least I didn't curse."

ABOUT THE AUTHOR

Varian Johnson is a writer and an engineer. He was born and raised in Florence, South Carolina, and attended the University of Oklahoma, where he received a B.S. in Civil Engineering. Varian is a member of the Society of Children's Book Writers and Illustrators, Words of Wisdom Writers' Society, and Alpha Phi Alpha Fraternity, Inc. Varian now lives in Austin, TX, with his wife, Crystal. *A Red Polka Dot In A World Full Of Plaid* is his first novel.

Excerpt from

A DRUMMER'S BEAT TO MEND

BY

KEI SWANSON

Release Date: November 2005

CHAPTER ONE

With a visible rhythm in his step, Tetsuro Takamitsu walked through the shadowy hallway behind the stage, his fingers tapping out the gentle cadence of his soul against his jean-encased thighs. A beat had always been there. It had been awakened by the pulse of rock and roll in cosmopolitan Tokyo, then refined by the tradition of feudal Japan and its ancient drummers.

Curtains at the wings swung, brushed by Tetsuro's fellow performers who arranged the drums on the stage for practice the next morning. The backstage area teemed with stagehands going about their work without regard to the Japanese performers helping them.

Whenever the group arrived early in the performance city, Tetsuro enjoyed taking in the city's sights instead of crashing at the hotel and seeing only the auditoriums. Taiko Nihon, the drummers' troupe, would give two night performances in Cleveland. He had the afternoons free to attend baseball games of the Cleveland Indians. Tetsuro was not alone in his passion for America's favorite pastime. No matter how far away from the shores of Japan her drummer-sons strayed, the lure and love of baseball was always present. The Japanese love for the game was renown, at times surpassing that of Americans. Tetsuro looked forward to seeing Kentaro Ikuta pitch for the first time since the phenomenal pitcher from Nagasaki had defected, as the Japanese press called it, to the U.S.

Pulling sunglasses from his jeans' hip pocket, Tetsuro unfolded them around his eyes and exited the theater. The fresh air was energizing after the four-hour plane flight. A gentle breeze stirred the loose strands of straight raven hair draping his neck and shoulders. He ran a hand through his hair as he paused to breathe in the scent of grass and flowers. The heavy hair settled back around his shoulders seconds later.

From behind him, a sultry feminine voice spoke, "*Ohayo, Te-chan.*"

"*Ohayo.*" Tetsuro turned to the petite woman in her late twenties who leaned against the wall beside the door. "Are you not supposed to be unpacking wardrobe?"

"I am taking a break." She pushed from the wall and dropped her cigarette.

Tetsuro wondered whom she thought she was fooling since she merely took the smoke in her mouth before almost immediately blowing it out. He was glad he'd given up the habit before he was twenty. *Man! Had it been twelve years?*

"I absolutely hate caring for those old-fashioned kimono! Have you been stuck with unpacking the drums?"

"It is my turn." Tetsuro kept walking and she fell into step with him.

"Are the truck drivers and stagehands not hired to unload the drums? I do not understand why we have to unload and unpack."

"It is so you respect every element of performing, from the work of the lowest to the highest."

"Yeah, yeah, yeah."

Tetsuro stopped and looked at the woman.

"Kifume-*san*, if you do not like it, why do you study? *Taiko* is an art…every part of it. If you can not respect one element, how can you honor another?"

Kifume snorted softly, then said, "You make it sound like a religion."

"It is…almost." With his rhythmic walk Tetsuro continued down the sidewalk toward the eighteen-wheeler backed to the curb.

"I like the performing!" Kifume trotted to catch up with him. "And, I like one of the drummers!"

"Well, *that* has been over for a while." It was Tetsuro's turn to scoff.

"Not soon enough." Kifume stopped moving.

Tetsuro took three more steps ahead of her, then halted. He'd heard such a tone before when he was twenty. He turned back to look over his shoulder, pulling his sunglasses down his nose to see her clearly.

"What do you mean?" He jerked the sunglasses off in anger.

"I am pregnant."

The tone *was* the same. Rage flooded through him.

"You said you were on the pill." Hadn't Emiko taught him not to be too trusting?

"So…I lied." Kifume stared straight at him as she spoke. At home, her eye contact would be considered bold. Japanese women, even in the twenty-first century, weren't brazen enough to confront a man thusly. Kifume's youth, exposure to America and its customs, and the familiarity grown from studying *taiko*, gave her the confidence to be so direct with him.

"We also used protection," he continued.

"Maybe it slipped." Kifume gave a slight shrug of her narrow shoulders.

Furious, Tetsuro turned on the heels of his black leather boots and stomped to the truck. The back door was open and half of the equipment was already in the theater. He hung his sunglasses by the earpiece in his back pocket and stepped into the dark cavern. At the midpoint sat a large crate with the *O-Daiko,* the largest drum, and the centerpiece of the show. He should have help to move it, but anger and ego clouded his judgment. Once he moved it to the end of the van, the others would be there to help.

Kifume followed. "Are you not going to say anything?"

"I think you have said enough for the moment. Besides, how do I know you are not lying now?" Tetsuro put his hands on the edge of the huge, heavy crate. "What makes you think it is mine? You *like* a lot of drummers."

He wiggled the crate forward. The rollers of the pallet below the large crate allowed it to move easily, almost on its own.

Kifume moved behind the crate and unhooked a strap.

"This will make it easier."

"No! I have had enough of your help." Too late Tetsuro's words ricocheted off the walls of the truck.

The great crate lunged, surging without warning toward the left. Tetsuro gripped the edges, spreading his feet apart to brace himself. Extending his arms wide, he clutched the rough planks with his long fingers, but his attempt to hold the heavy object in place was futile. The crate shifted in the unleveled truck and the edge of the heavy box slammed his left hand into the truck wall. Monstrous pain ripped through his arm and his deep-throated scream echoed in the cavernous truck.

"Tetsu!" Kifume threw her slight weight against the crate. Unable to move it, she clutched the rope strung across the back and pulled. Still unable to relieve any of the pressure on Tetsuro's hand, she shouted in English, "Help! Somebody! Help!"

"What the…?" The returning driver jumped into the truck and grasped one side of the large crate and heaved.

More performers arrived, returning to continue unloading the truck. Seeing the situation, some of them rushed to shove the drum crate away while others bent over Tetsuro. His hand was pinned between the crate and the wall four feet above the truck floor. His body turned into the side of van. Pain ran from his fingers to his shoulder and echoed in his chest with the bounding beat of his blood. His scream gargled back into his throat as intense agony took all the breath from him.

Once the pressure was removed, Tetsuro slid down the wall. Folding his legs beneath him on the floor, he cradled his left hand in his right. Blood throbbed to the injury in a painful rush and a nauseous knot balled up in his stomach, threatening to force the airline meal up. He fought the wave of sickness and struggled not to lose consciousness.

"*Te-chan, sumimasen.*" Kifume wept as she reached toward his hand.

"Get away from me!" he growled, refusing her apology.

"We need to get you to a hospital," said a male performer who kneeled to help Tetsuro when Kifume moved away.

"I think you are right, Susu-*san.*" Tetsuro battled the pain striving to overtake his consciousness.

Susumu, his best friend, put a supporting arm around his back and helped him stand as Tetsuro held the injured hand higher than his fast pounding heart. He'd already discovered that blood flowing downward increased the pain.

"What about the performance?" Tetsuro groaned, his voice barely audible.

"Do not worry. We will get along without our beloved artistic manager," Susumu ribbed him. "While we are drumming before a nameless audience, you will be making new friends."

"Are you trying to make me feel better?" Tetsuro attempted a smile, but the cutting pain made it difficult.

"Trying to, my friend."

Leave it to Susumu to see the bright side of things. Tetsuro leaned heavily on his friend, happy to have the support. Who knew what the next few hours would bring, much less the following day?

2005 Publication Schedule

January

A Heart's Awakening	Falling
Veronica Parker	Natalie Dunbar
$9.95	$9.95
1-58571-143-8	1-58571-121-7

February

Echoes of Yesterday	A Love of Her Own	Higher Ground
Beverly Clark	Cheris F. Hodges	Leah Latimer
$9.95	$9.95	$19.95
1-58571-131-4	1-58571-136-5	1-58571-157-8

March

Misconceptions	I'll Paint a Sun	Peace Be Still
Pamela Leigh Starr	A.J. Garrotto	Colette Haywood
$9.95	$9.95	$12.95
1-58571-117-9	1-58571-165-9	1-58571-129-2

April

Intentional Mistakes	Conquering Dr. Wexler's Heart	Song in the Park
Michele Sudler	Kimberley White	Martin Brant
$9.95	$9.95	$15.95
1-58571-152-7	1-58571-126-8	1-58571-125-X

May

The Color Line	Unconditional	Last Train to Memphis
Lizzette Grayson Carter	A.C. Arthur	Elsa Cook
$9.95	$9.95	$12.95
1-58571-163-2	1-58571-142-X	1-58571-146-2

June

Angel's Paradise	Suddenly You	Matters of Life and Death
Janice Angelique	Crystal Hubbard	Lesego Malepe, Ph.D.
$9.95	$9.95	$15.95
1-58571-107-1	1-58571-158-6	1-58571-124-1

2005 Publication Schedule (continued)

July

Class Reunion
Irma Jenkins/John
  Brown
$12.95
1-58571-123-3

Wild Ravens
Altonya Washington
$9.95
1-58571-164-0

August

Path of Thorns
Annetta P. Lee
$9.95
1-58571-145-4

Timeless Devotion
Bella McFarland
$9.95
1-58571-148-9

Life Is Never As It Seems
J.J. Michael
$12.95
1-58571-153-5

September

Beyond the Rapture
Beverly Clark
$9.95
1-58571-130-6

Blood Lust
J. M. Jeffries
$9.95
1-58571-138-1

Rough on Rats and
  Tough on Cats
Chris Parker
$12.95
1-58571-154-3

October

A Will to Love
Angie Daniels
$9.95
1-58571-141-1

Taken by You
Dorothy Elizabeth Love
$9.95
1-58571-162-4

Soul Eyes
Wayne L. Wilson
$12.95
1-58571-147-0

November

A Drummer's Beat to
  Mend
Kei Swanson
$9.95
1-58571-171-3

Sweet Reprecussions
Kimberley White
$9.95
1-58571-159-4

Red Polka Dot in a
  World of Plaid
Varian Johnson
$12.95
1-58571-140-3

December

Hand in Glove
Andrea Jackson
$9.95
1-58571-166-7

Blaze
Barbara Keaton
$9.95
1-58571-172-1

Across
Carol Payne
$12.95
1-58571-149-7

Other Genesis Press, Inc. Titles

Acquisitions	Kimberley White	$8.95
A Dangerous Deception	J.M. Jeffries	$8.95
A Dangerous Love	J.M. Jeffries	$8.95
A Dangerous Obsession	J.M. Jeffries	$8.95
After the Vows	Leslie Esdaile	$10.95
(Summer Anthology)	T.T. Henderson	
	Jacqueline Thomas	
Again My Love	Kayla Perrin	$10.95
Against the Wind	Gwynne Forster	$8.95
A Lark on the Wing	Phyliss Hamilton	$8.95
A Lighter Shade of Brown	Vicki Andrews	$8.95
All I Ask	Barbara Keaton	$8.95
A Love to Cherish	Beverly Clark	$8.95
Ambrosia	T.T. Henderson	$8.95
And Then Came You	Dorothy Elizabeth Love	$8.95
Angel's Paradise	Janice Angelique	$8.95
A Risk of Rain	Dar Tomlinson	$8.95
At Last	Lisa G. Riley	$8.95
Best of Friends	Natalie Dunbar	$8.95
Bound by Love	Beverly Clark	$8.95
Breeze	Robin Hampton Allen	$10.95
Brown Sugar Diaries &	Delores Bundy &	$10.95
Other Sexy Tales	Cole Riley	
By Design	Barbara Keaton	$8.95
Cajun Heat	Charlene Berry	$8.95
Careless Whispers	Rochelle Alers	$8.95
Caught in a Trap	Andre Michelle	$8.95
Chances	Pamela Leigh Starr	$8.95
Dark Embrace	Crystal Wilson Harris	$8.95
Dark Storm Rising	Chinelu Moore	$10.95
Designer Passion	Dar Tomlinson	$8.95
Ebony Butterfly II	Delilah Dawson	$14.95

Erotic Anthology	Assorted	$8.95
Eve's Prescription	Edwina Martin Arnold	$8.95
Everlastin' Love	Gay G. Gunn	$8.95
Fate	Pamela Leigh Starr	$8.95
Forbidden Quest	Dar Tomlinson	$10.95
Fragment in the Sand	Annetta P. Lee	$8.95
From the Ashes	Kathleen Suzanne	$8.95
	Jeanne Sumerix	
Gentle Yearning	Rochelle Alers	$10.95
Glory of Love	Sinclair LeBeau	$10.95
Hart & Soul	Angie Daniels	$8.95
Heartbeat	Stephanie Bedwell-Grime	$8.95
I'll Be Your Shelter	Giselle Carmichael	$8.95
Illusions	Pamela Leigh Starr	$8.95
Indiscretions	Donna Hill	$8.95
Interlude	Donna Hill	$8.95
Intimate Intentions	Angie Daniels	$8.95
Just an Affair	Eugenia O'Neal	$8.95
Kiss or Keep	Debra Phillips	$8.95
Love Always	Mildred E. Riley	$10.95
Love Unveiled	Gloria Greene	$10.95
Love's Deception	Charlene Berry	$10.95
Mae's Promise	Melody Walcott	$8.95
Meant to Be	Jeanne Sumerix	$8.95
Midnight Clear	Leslie Esdaile	$10.95
(Anthology)	Gwynne Forster	
	Carmen Green	
	Monica Jackson	
Midnight Magic	Gwynne Forster	$8.95
Midnight Peril	Vicki Andrews	$10.95
My Buffalo Soldier	Barbara B. K. Reeves	$8.95
Naked Soul	Gwynne Forster	$8.95
No Regrets	Mildred E. Riley	$8.95
Nowhere to Run	Gay G. Gunn	$10.95

Object of His Desire	A. C. Arthur	$8.95
One Day at a Time	Bella McFarland	$8.95
Passion	T.T. Henderson	$10.95
Past Promises	Jahmel West	$8.95
Path of Fire	T.T. Henderson	$8.95
Picture Perfect	Reon Carter	$8.95
Pride & Joi	Gay G. Gunn	$8.95
Quiet Storm	Donna Hill	$8.95
Reckless Surrender	Rochelle Alers	$8.95
Rendezvous with Fate	Jeanne Sumerix	$8.95
Revelations	Cheris F. Hodges	$8.95
Rivers of the Soul	Leslie Esdaile	$8.95
Rooms of the Heart	Donna Hill	$8.95
Shades of Brown	Denise Becker	$8.95
Shades of Desire	Monica White	$8.95
Sin	Crystal Rhodes	$8.95
So Amazing	Sinclair LeBeau	$8.95
Somebody's Someone	Sinclair LeBeau	$8.95
Someone to Love	Alicia Wiggins	$8.95
Soul to Soul	Donna Hill	$8.95
Still Waters Run Deep	Leslie Esdaile	$8.95
Subtle Secrets	Wanda Y. Thomas	$8.95
Sweet Tomorrows	Kimberly White	$8.95
The Color of Trouble	Dyanne Davis	$8.95
The Price of Love	Sinclair LeBeau	$8.95
The Reluctant Captive	Joyce Jackson	$8.95
The Missing Link	Charlyne Dickerson	$8.95
Three Wishes	Seressia Glass	$8.95
Tomorrow's Promise	Leslie Esdaile	$8.95
Truly Inseperable	Wanda Y. Thomas	$8.95
Twist of Fate	Beverly Clark	$8.95
Unbreak My Heart	Dar Tomlinson	$8.95
Unconditional Love	Alicia Wiggins	$8.95
When Dreams A Float	Dorothy Elizabeth Love	$8.95

Whispers in the Night	Dorothy Elizabeth Love	$8.95
Whispers in the Sand	LaFlorya Gauthier	$10.95
Yesterday is Gone	Beverly Clark	$8.95
Yesterday's Dreams, Tomorrow's Promises	Reon Laudat	$8.95
Your Precious Love	Sinclair LeBeau	$8.95

Order Form

Mail to: Genesis Press, Inc.
P.O. Box 101
Columbus, MS 39703

Name _____

Address _____

City/State _____ Zip _____

Telephone _____

Ship to (if different from above)

Name _____

Address _____

City/State _____ Zip _____

Telephone _____

Credit Card Information

Credit Card # _____ ☐ Visa   ☐ Mastercard

Expiration Date (mm/yy) _____ ☐ AmEx   ☐ Discover

Qty.	Author	Title	Price	Total

Use this order form, or call

1-888-INDIGO-1

Total for books _____

Shipping and handling:
  $5 first two books,
  $1 each additional book _____

Total S & H _____

Total amount enclosed _____

Mississippi residents add 7% sales tax